ASTERIX
THE GLADIATOR

TEXT BY GOSCINNY

DRAWINGS BY UDERZO

TRANSLATED BY ANTHEA BELL AND DEREK HOCKRIDGE

DARGAUD PUBLISHING INTERNATIONAL, LTD.

© DARGAUD EDITEUR PARIS 1964
© HODDER & STOUGHTON LTD. 1969
for the English language text

ISBN 0-917201-55-8

Exclusive licenced distributor for USA:

Distribooks Inc.
8220 N. Christiana Ave.
Skokie, IL 60076-2911
Tel: (708) 676-1596
Fax: (708) 676-1195
Toll-free fax: 800-433-9229

Imprimé en France-Publiphotoffset 93500 Pantin-en mars 1995

Printed in France

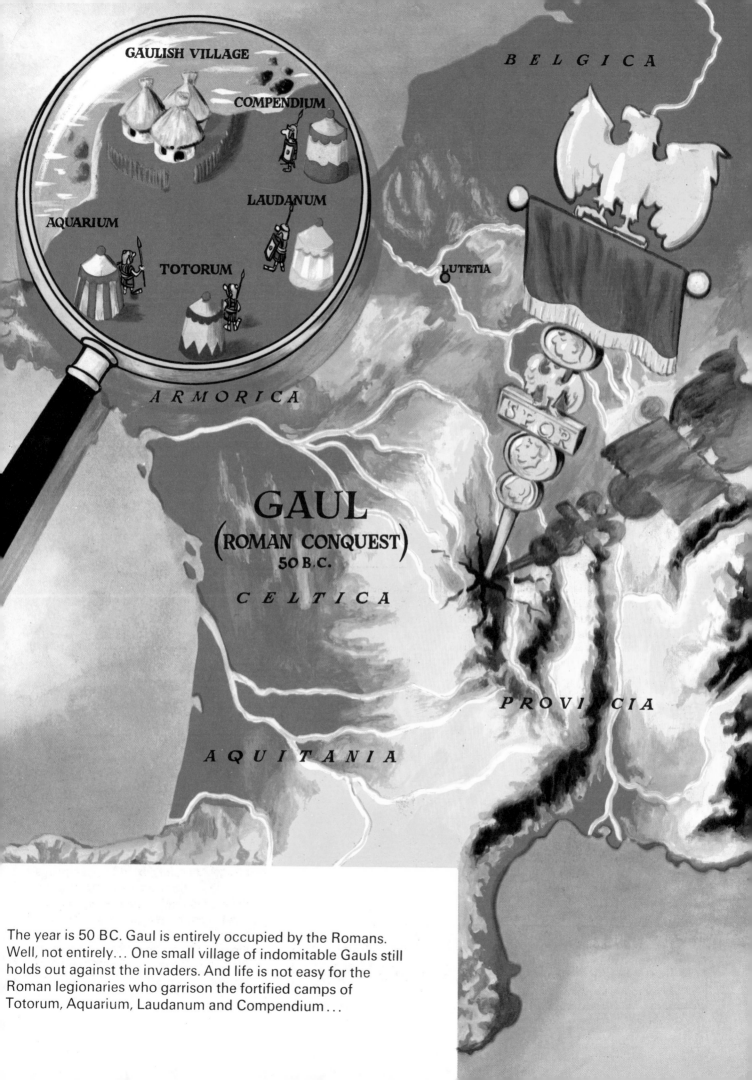

GAULISH VILLAGE

COMPENDIUM

LAUDANUM

AQUARIUM

TOTORUM

ARMORICA

BELGICA

LUTETIA

SPQR

GAUL
(ROMAN CONQUEST)
50 B.C.

CELTICA

PROVINCIA

AQUITANIA

The year is 50 BC. Gaul is entirely occupied by the Romans. Well, not entirely… One small village of indomitable Gauls still holds out against the invaders. And life is not easy for the Roman legionaries who garrison the fortified camps of Totorum, Aquarium, Laudanum and Compendium…

a few of the Gauls ...

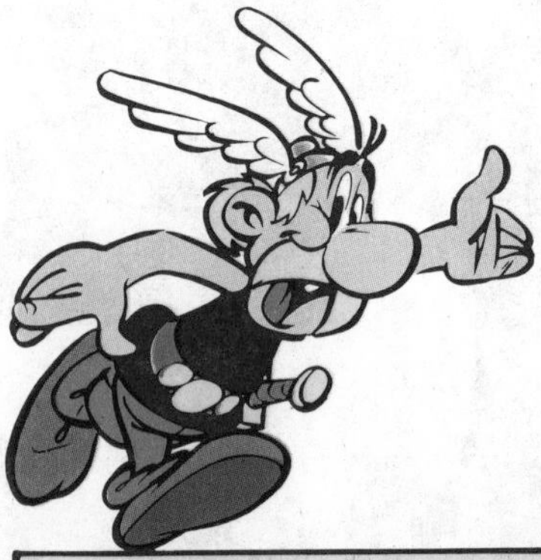

Asterix, the hero of these adventures. A shrewd, cunning little warrior; all perilous missions are immediately entrusted to him. Asterix gets his superhuman strength from the magic potion brewed by the druid Getafix...

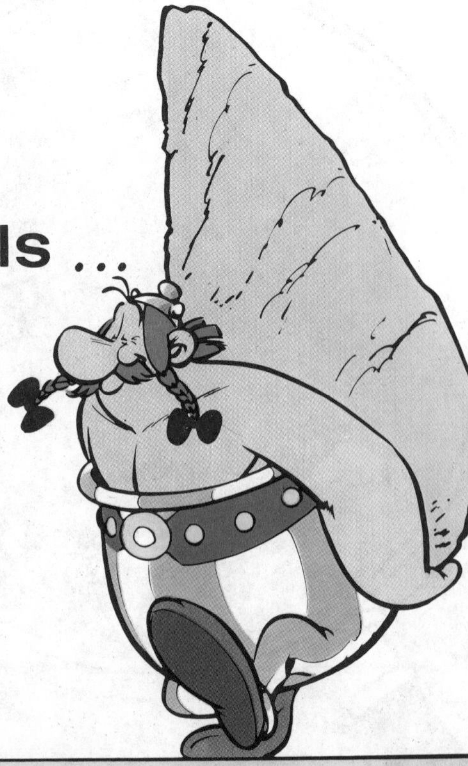

Obelix, Asterix's inseparable friend. A menhir delivery-man by trade; addicted to wild boar. Obelix is always ready to drop everything and go off on a new adventure with Asterix – so long as there's wild boar to eat, and plenty of fighting.

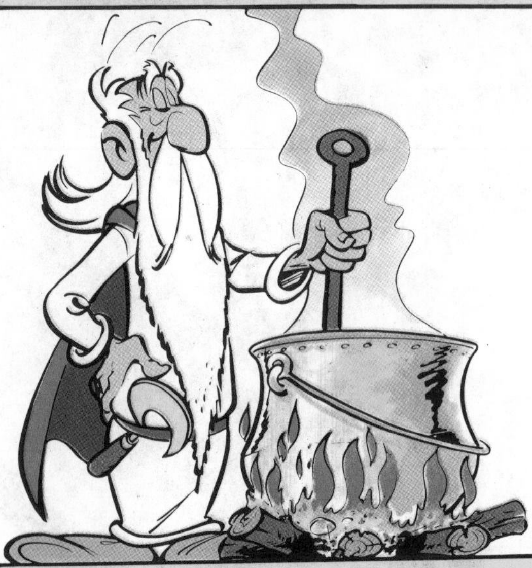

Getafix, the venerable village druid. Gathers mistletoe and brews magic potions. His speciality is the potion which gives the drinker superhuman strength. But Getafix also has other recipes up his sleeve...

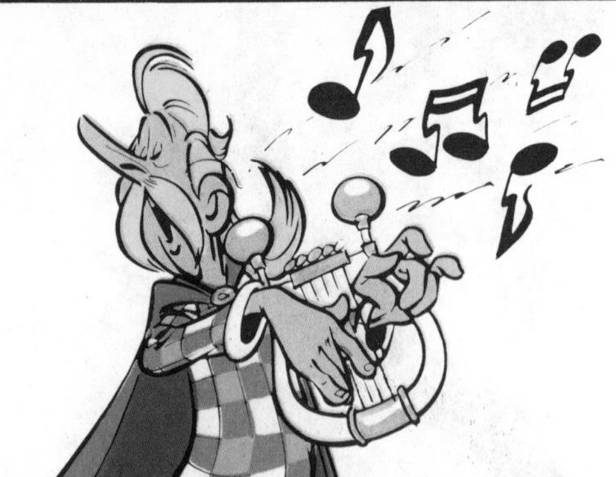

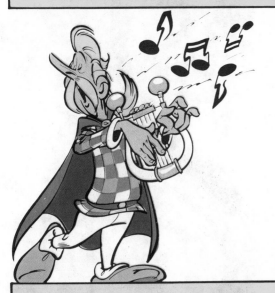

Cacofonix, the bard. Opinion is divided as to his musical gifts. Cacofonix thinks he's a genius. Everyone else thinks he's unspeakable. But so long as he doesn't speak, let alone sing, everybody likes him...

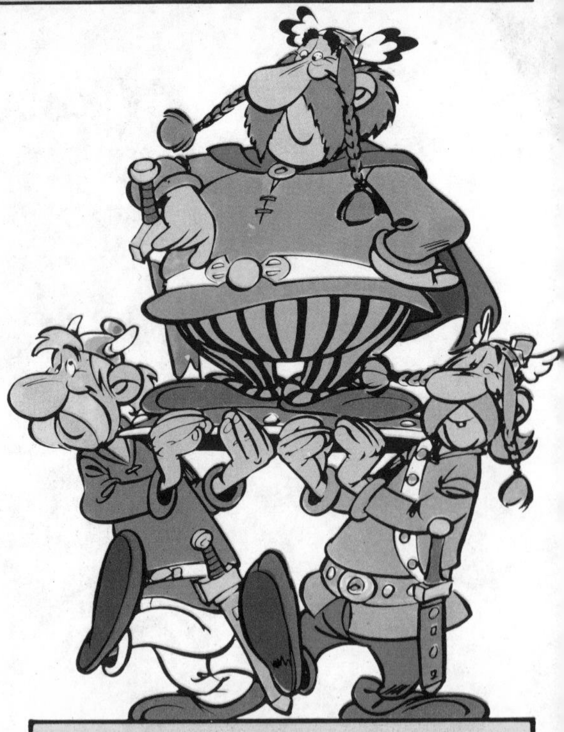

Finally, Vitalstatistix, the chief of the tribe. Majestic, brave and hot-tempered, the old warrior is respected by his men and feared by his enemies. Vitalstatistix himself has only one fear; he is afraid the sky may fall on his head tomorrow. But as he always says, 'Tomorrow never comes.

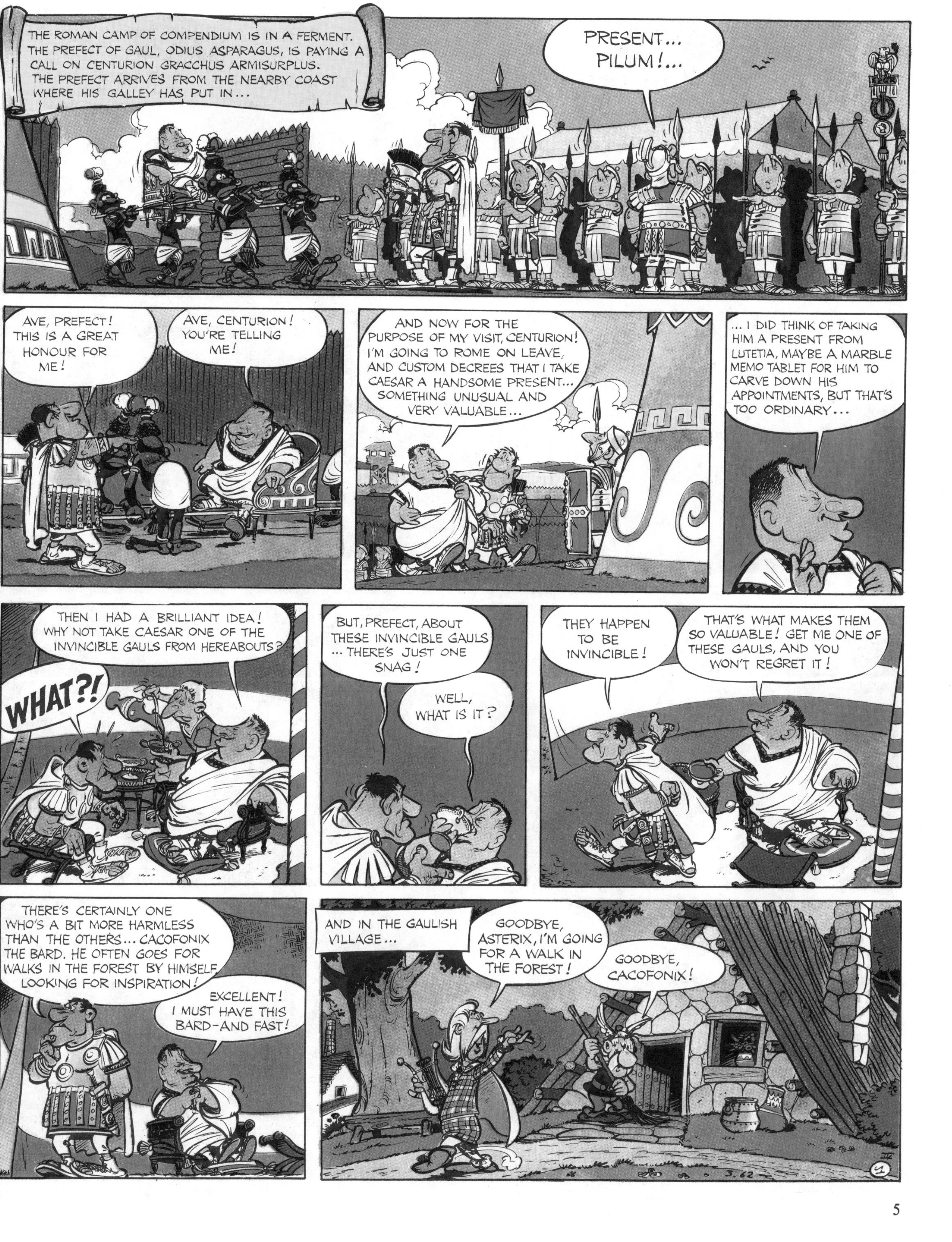
THE ROMAN CAMP OF COMPENDIUM IS IN A FERMENT. THE PREFECT OF GAUL, ODIUS ASPARAGUS, IS PAYING A CALL ON CENTURION GRACCHUS ARMISURPLUS. THE PREFECT ARRIVES FROM THE NEARBY COAST WHERE HIS GALLEY HAS PUT IN...
PRESENT... PILUM!...
AVE, PREFECT! THIS IS A GREAT HONOUR FOR ME!
AVE, CENTURION! YOU'RE TELLING ME!
AND NOW FOR THE PURPOSE OF MY VISIT, CENTURION! I'M GOING TO ROME ON LEAVE, AND CUSTOM DECREES THAT I TAKE CAESAR A HANDSOME PRESENT... SOMETHING UNUSUAL AND VERY VALUABLE...
... I DID THINK OF TAKING HIM A PRESENT FROM LUTETIA, MAYBE A MARBLE MEMO TABLET FOR HIM TO CARVE DOWN HIS APPOINTMENTS, BUT THAT'S TOO ORDINARY...
THEN I HAD A BRILLIANT IDEA! WHY NOT TAKE CAESAR ONE OF THE INVINCIBLE GAULS FROM HEREABOUTS?
WHAT?!
BUT, PREFECT, ABOUT THESE INVINCIBLE GAULS ... THERE'S JUST ONE SNAG!
WELL, WHAT IS IT?
THEY HAPPEN TO BE INVINCIBLE!
THAT'S WHAT MAKES THEM SO VALUABLE! GET ME ONE OF THESE GAULS, AND YOU WON'T REGRET IT!
THERE'S CERTAINLY ONE WHO'S A BIT MORE HARMLESS THAN THE OTHERS... CACOFONIX THE BARD. HE OFTEN GOES FOR WALKS IN THE FOREST BY HIMSELF LOOKING FOR INSPIRATION!
EXCELLENT! I MUST HAVE THIS BARD-AND FAST!
AND IN THE GAULISH VILLAGE...
GOODBYE, ASTERIX, I'M GOING FOR A WALK IN THE FOREST!
GOODBYE, CACOFONIX!
3.62

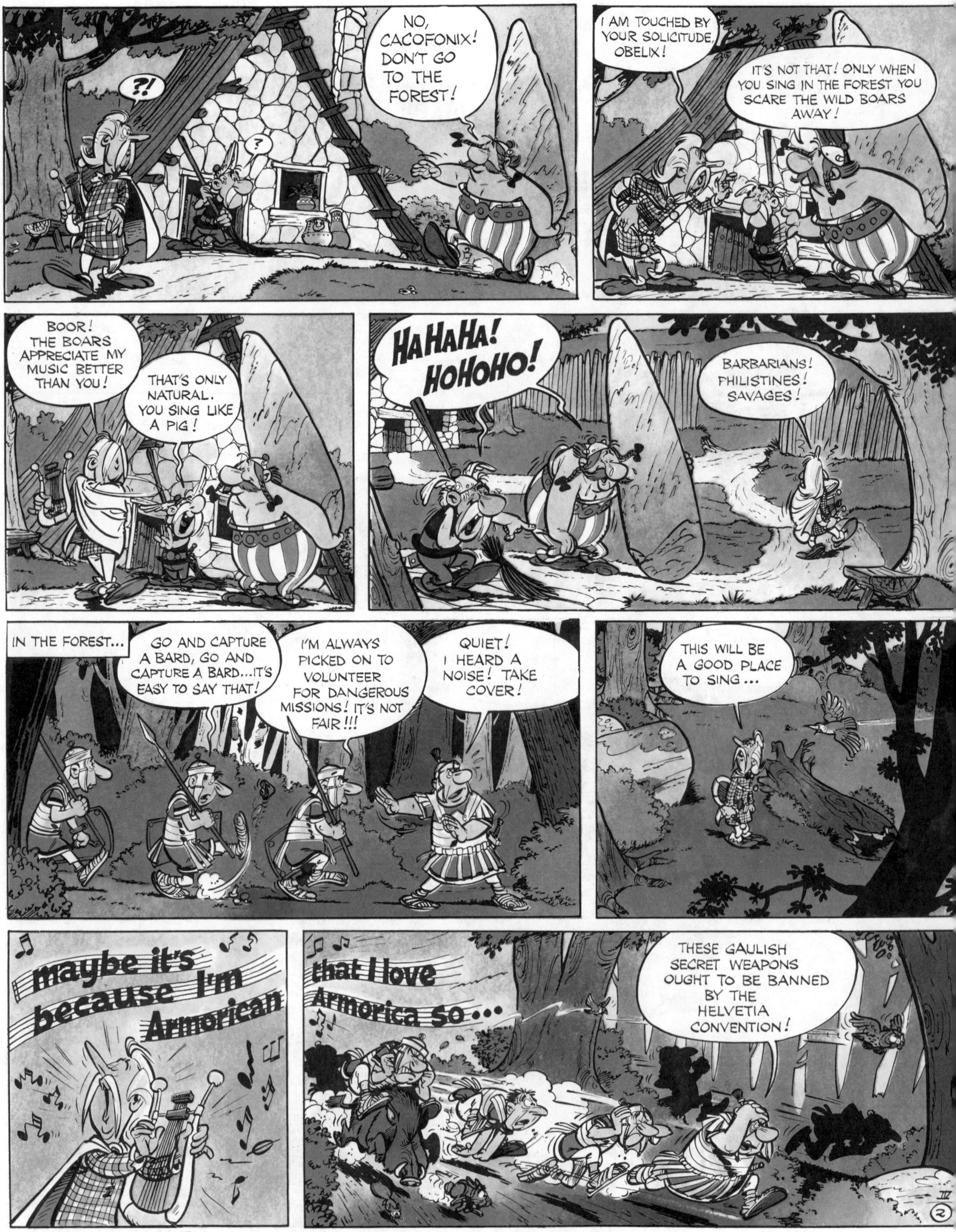
?!
?
NO, CACOFONIX! DON'T GO TO THE FOREST!
I AM TOUCHED BY YOUR SOLICITUDE, OBELIX!
IT'S NOT THAT! ONLY WHEN YOU SING IN THE FOREST YOU SCARE THE WILD BOARS AWAY!
BOOR! THE BOARS APPRECIATE MY MUSIC BETTER THAN YOU!
THAT'S ONLY NATURAL. YOU SING LIKE A PIG!
HAHAHA! HOHOHO!
BARBARIANS! PHILISTINES! SAVAGES!
IN THE FOREST...
GO AND CAPTURE A BARD, GO AND CAPTURE A BARD...IT'S EASY TO SAY THAT!
I'M ALWAYS PICKED ON TO VOLUNTEER FOR DANGEROUS MISSIONS! IT'S NOT FAIR!!!
QUIET! I HEARD A NOISE! TAKE COVER!
THIS WILL BE A GOOD PLACE TO SING...
maybe it's because I'm Armorican
that I love Armorica so...
THESE GAULISH SECRET WEAPONS OUGHT TO BE BANNED BY THE HELVETIA CONVENTION!

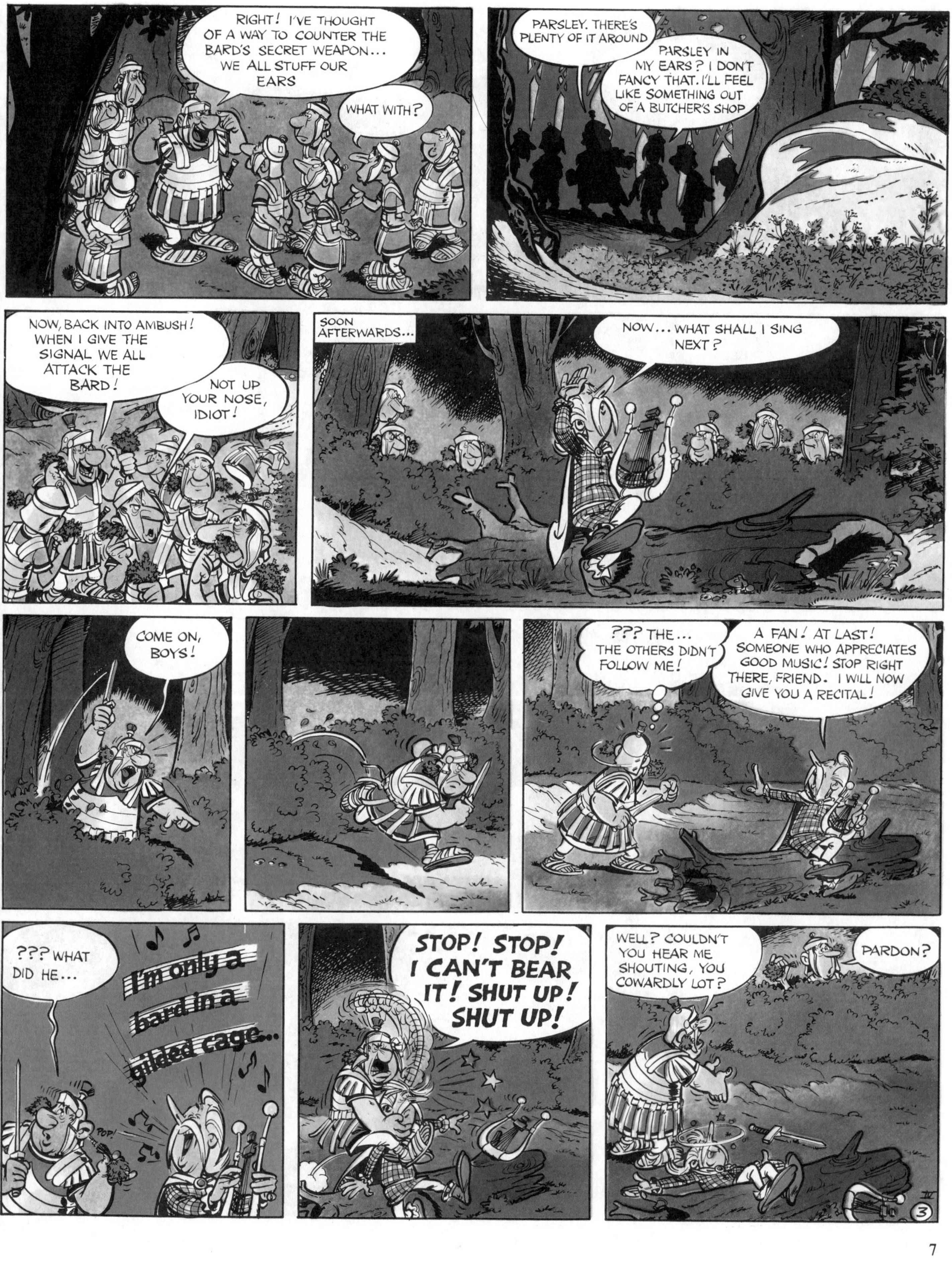
RIGHT! I'VE THOUGHT OF A WAY TO COUNTER THE BARD'S SECRET WEAPON... WE ALL STUFF OUR EARS
WHAT WITH?
PARSLEY. THERE'S PLENTY OF IT AROUND
PARSLEY IN MY EARS? I DON'T FANCY THAT. I'LL FEEL LIKE SOMETHING OUT OF A BUTCHER'S SHOP
NOW, BACK INTO AMBUSH! WHEN I GIVE THE SIGNAL WE ALL ATTACK THE BARD!
NOT UP YOUR NOSE, IDIOT!
SOON AFTERWARDS...
NOW... WHAT SHALL I SING NEXT?
COME ON, BOYS!
??? THE... THE OTHERS DIDN'T FOLLOW ME!
A FAN! AT LAST! SOMEONE WHO APPRECIATES GOOD MUSIC! STOP RIGHT THERE, FRIEND. I WILL NOW GIVE YOU A RECITAL!
??? WHAT DID HE...
I'm only a bard in a gilded cage...
POP!
STOP! STOP! I CAN'T BEAR IT! SHUT UP! SHUT UP!
WELL? COULDN'T YOU HEAR ME SHOUTING, YOU COWARDLY LOT?
PARDON?
IV
3

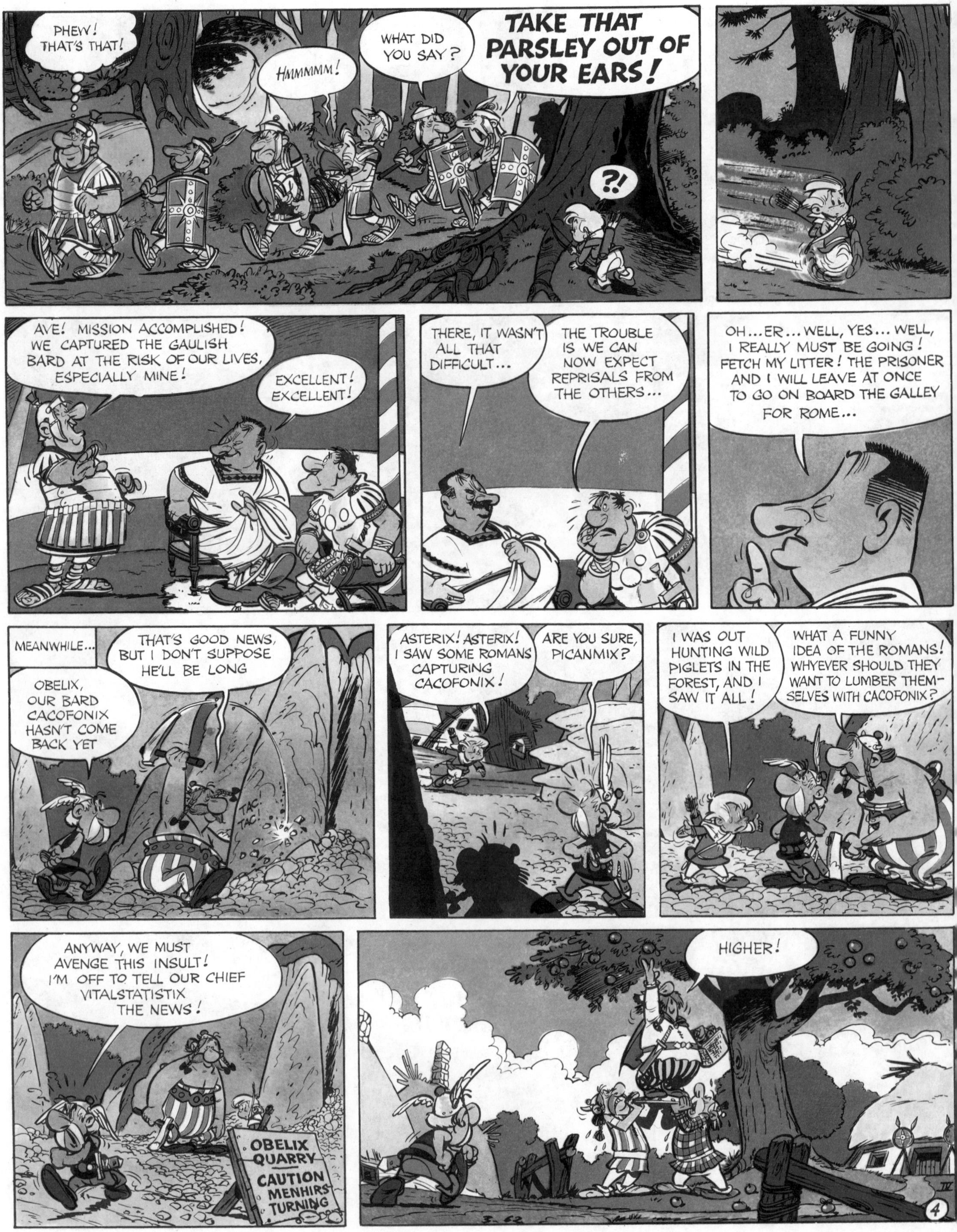
PHEW! THAT'S THAT!
HMMMMM!
WHAT DID YOU SAY?
TAKE THAT PARSLEY OUT OF YOUR EARS!
?!
AVE! MISSION ACCOMPLISHED! WE CAPTURED THE GAULISH BARD AT THE RISK OF OUR LIVES, ESPECIALLY MINE!
EXCELLENT! EXCELLENT!
THERE, IT WASN'T ALL THAT DIFFICULT...
THE TROUBLE IS WE CAN NOW EXPECT REPRISALS FROM THE OTHERS...
OH... ER... WELL, YES... WELL, I REALLY MUST BE GOING! FETCH MY LITTER! THE PRISONER AND I WILL LEAVE AT ONCE TO GO ON BOARD THE GALLEY FOR ROME...
MEANWHILE...
OBELIX, OUR BARD CACOFONIX HASN'T COME BACK YET
THAT'S GOOD NEWS, BUT I DON'T SUPPOSE HE'LL BE LONG
TAC TAC
ASTERIX! ASTERIX! I SAW SOME ROMANS CAPTURING CACOFONIX!
ARE YOU SURE, PICANMIX?
I WAS OUT HUNTING WILD PIGLETS IN THE FOREST, AND I SAW IT ALL!
WHAT A FUNNY IDEA OF THE ROMANS! WHYEVER SHOULD THEY WANT TO LUMBER THEMSELVES WITH CACOFONIX?
ANYWAY, WE MUST AVENGE THIS INSULT! I'M OFF TO TELL OUR CHIEF VITALSTATISTIX THE NEWS!
OBELIX QUARRY
CAUTION MENHIRS TURNING
HIGHER!
4

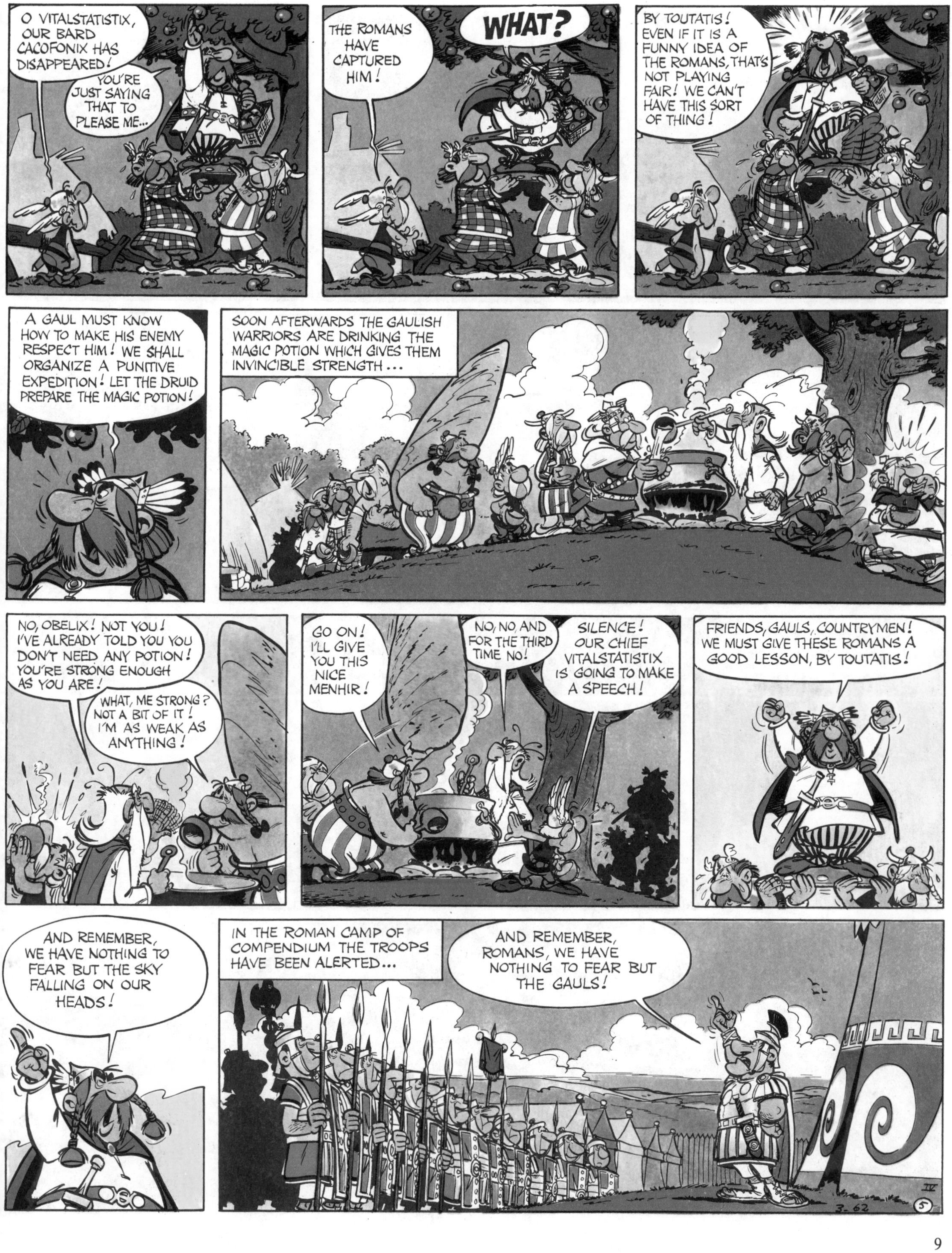
O VITALSTATISTIX, OUR BARD CACOFONIX HAS DISAPPEARED!
YOU'RE JUST SAYING THAT TO PLEASE ME...
THE ROMANS HAVE CAPTURED HIM!
WHAT?
BY TOUTATIS! EVEN IF IT IS A FUNNY IDEA OF THE ROMANS, THAT'S NOT PLAYING FAIR! WE CAN'T HAVE THIS SORT OF THING!
A GAUL MUST KNOW HOW TO MAKE HIS ENEMY RESPECT HIM! WE SHALL ORGANIZE A PUNITIVE EXPEDITION! LET THE DRUID PREPARE THE MAGIC POTION!
SOON AFTERWARDS THE GAULISH WARRIORS ARE DRINKING THE MAGIC POTION WHICH GIVES THEM INVINCIBLE STRENGTH...
NO, OBELIX! NOT YOU! I'VE ALREADY TOLD YOU YOU DON'T NEED ANY POTION! YOU'RE STRONG ENOUGH AS YOU ARE!
WHAT, ME STRONG? NOT A BIT OF IT! I'M AS WEAK AS ANYTHING!
GO ON! I'LL GIVE YOU THIS NICE MENHIR!
NO, NO, AND FOR THE THIRD TIME NO!
SILENCE! OUR CHIEF VITALSTATISTIX IS GOING TO MAKE A SPEECH!
FRIENDS, GAULS, COUNTRYMEN! WE MUST GIVE THESE ROMANS A GOOD LESSON, BY TOUTATIS!
AND REMEMBER, WE HAVE NOTHING TO FEAR BUT THE SKY FALLING ON OUR HEADS!
IN THE ROMAN CAMP OF COMPENDIUM THE TROOPS HAVE BEEN ALERTED...
AND REMEMBER, ROMANS, WE HAVE NOTHING TO FEAR BUT THE GAULS!

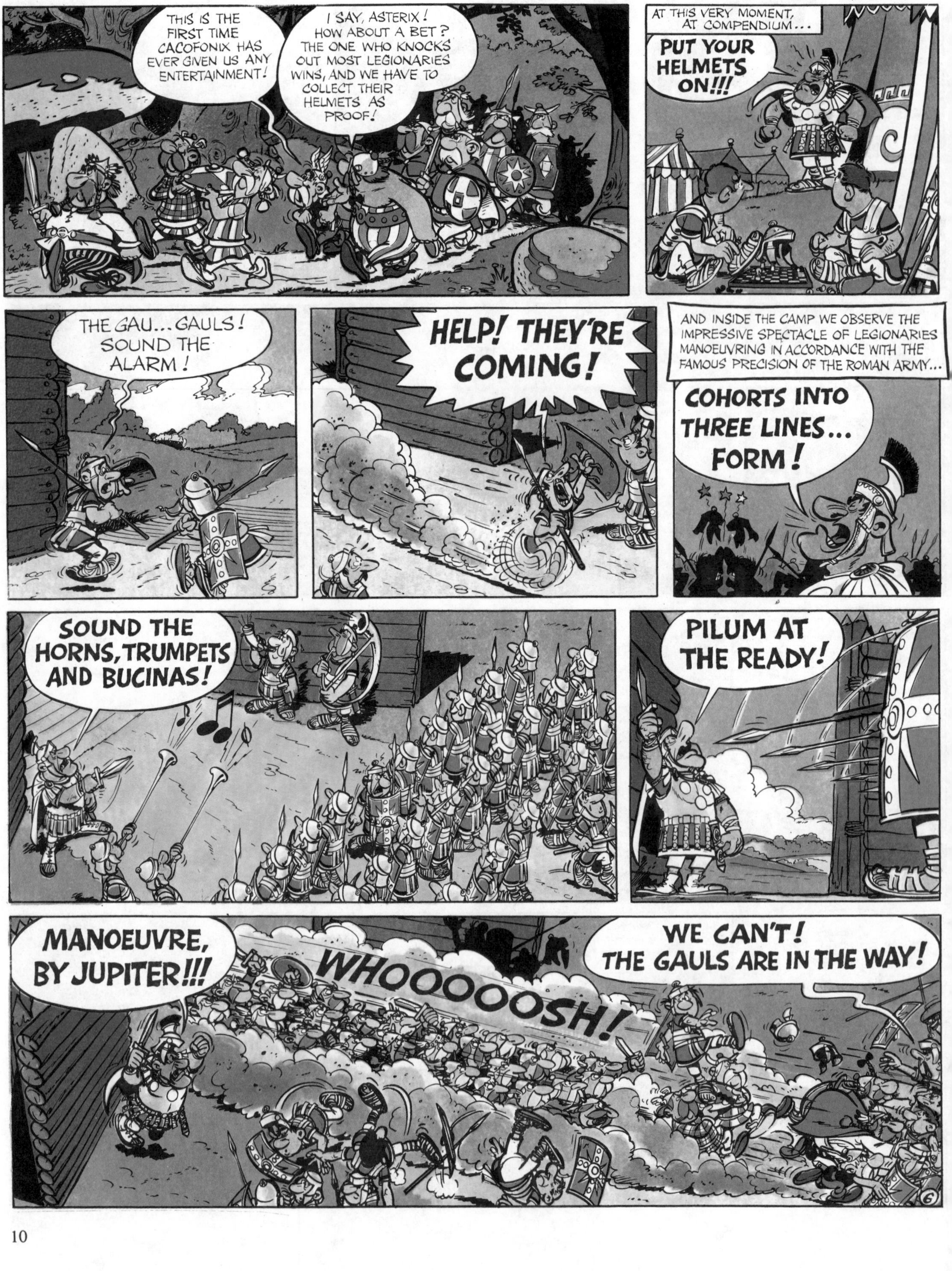

THIS IS THE FIRST TIME CACOFONIX HAS EVER GIVEN US ANY ENTERTAINMENT!
I SAY, ASTERIX! HOW ABOUT A BET? THE ONE WHO KNOCKS OUT MOST LEGIONARIES WINS, AND WE HAVE TO COLLECT THEIR HELMETS AS PROOF!
AT THIS VERY MOMENT, AT COMPENDIUM...
PUT YOUR HELMETS ON!!!
THE GAU... GAULS! SOUND THE ALARM!
HELP! THEY'RE COMING!
AND INSIDE THE CAMP WE OBSERVE THE IMPRESSIVE SPECTACLE OF LEGIONARIES MANOEUVRING IN ACCORDANCE WITH THE FAMOUS PRECISION OF THE ROMAN ARMY...
COHORTS INTO THREE LINES... FORM!
SOUND THE HORNS, TRUMPETS AND BUCINAS!
PILUM AT THE READY!
MANOEUVRE, BY JUPITER!!!
WHOOOOOOSH!
WE CAN'T! THE GAULS ARE IN THE WAY!
6

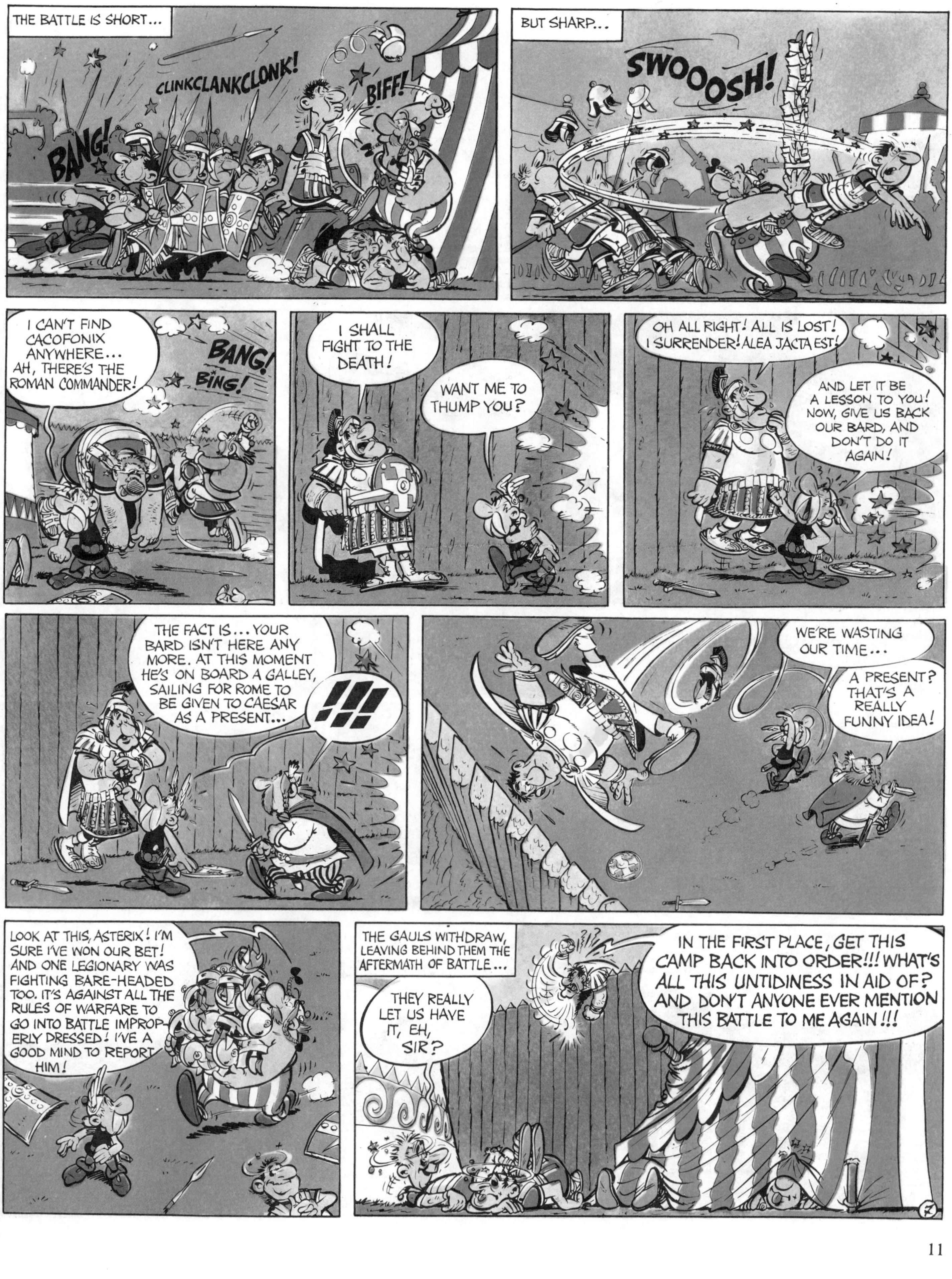

THE BATTLE IS SHORT...
CLINKCLANKCLONK!
BIFF!
BANG!
BUT SHARP...
SWOOOSH!
I CAN'T FIND CACOFONIX ANYWHERE... AH, THERE'S THE ROMAN COMMANDER!
BANG!
BING!
I SHALL FIGHT TO THE DEATH!
WANT ME TO THUMP YOU?
OH ALL RIGHT! ALL IS LOST! I SURRENDER! ALEA JACTA EST!
AND LET IT BE A LESSON TO YOU! NOW, GIVE US BACK OUR BARD, AND DON'T DO IT AGAIN!
THE FACT IS... YOUR BARD ISN'T HERE ANY MORE. AT THIS MOMENT HE'S ON BOARD A GALLEY, SAILING FOR ROME TO BE GIVEN TO CAESAR AS A PRESENT...
!!!
WE'RE WASTING OUR TIME...
A PRESENT? THAT'S A REALLY FUNNY IDEA!
LOOK AT THIS, ASTERIX! I'M SURE I'VE WON OUR BET! AND ONE LEGIONARY WAS FIGHTING BARE-HEADED TOO. IT'S AGAINST ALL THE RULES OF WARFARE TO GO INTO BATTLE IMPROPERLY DRESSED! I'VE A GOOD MIND TO REPORT HIM!
THE GAULS WITHDRAW, LEAVING BEHIND THEM THE AFTERMATH OF BATTLE...
THEY REALLY LET US HAVE IT, EH, SIR?
IN THE FIRST PLACE, GET THIS CAMP BACK INTO ORDER!!! WHAT'S ALL THIS UNTIDINESS IN AID OF? AND DON'T ANYONE EVER MENTION THIS BATTLE TO ME AGAIN!!!

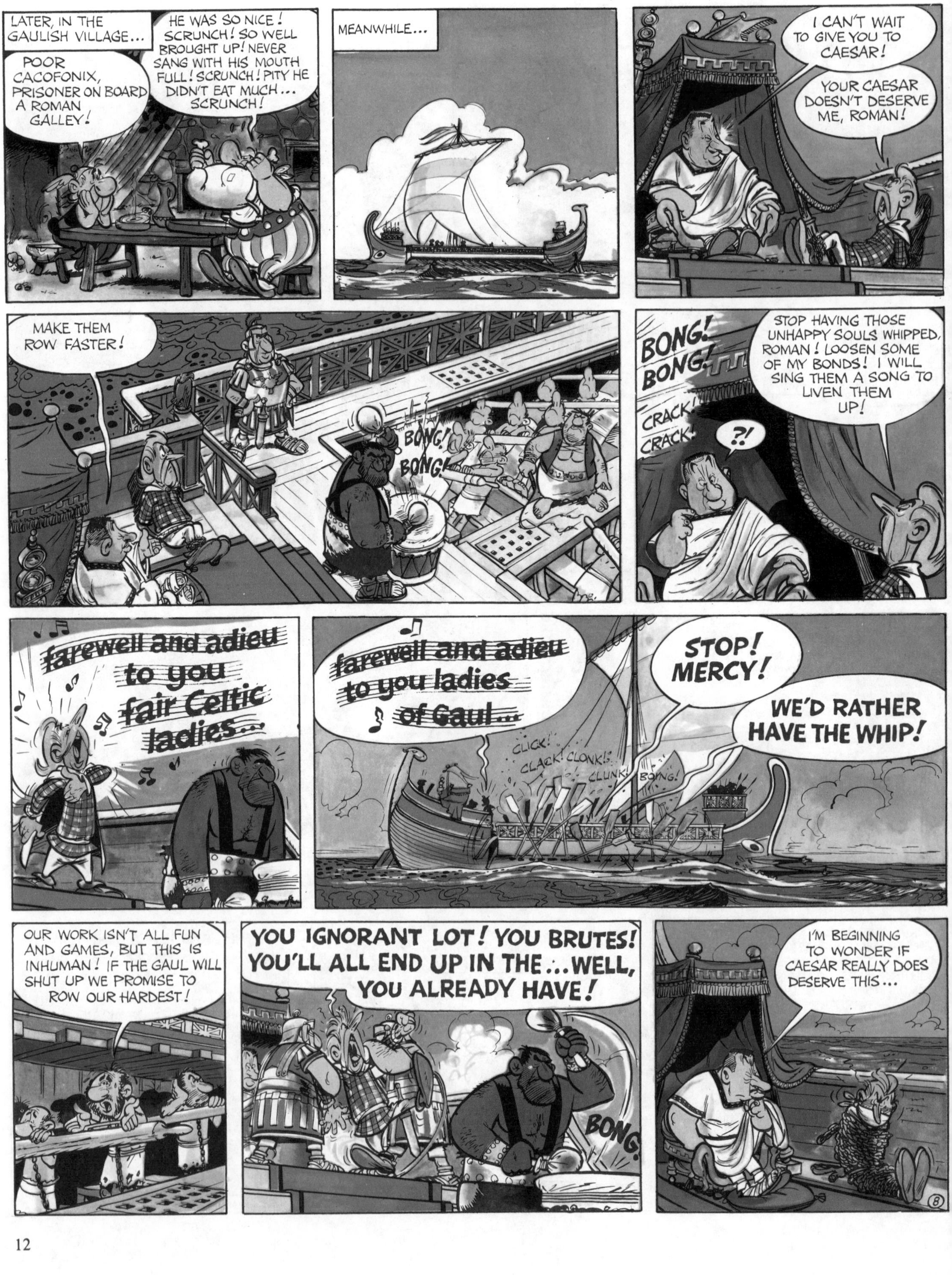

LATER, IN THE GAULISH VILLAGE...
POOR CACOFONIX, PRISONER ON BOARD A ROMAN GALLEY!
HE WAS SO NICE! SCRUNCH! SO WELL BROUGHT UP! NEVER SANG WITH HIS MOUTH FULL! SCRUNCH! PITY HE DIDN'T EAT MUCH... SCRUNCH!
MEANWHILE...
I CAN'T WAIT TO GIVE YOU TO CAESAR!
YOUR CAESAR DOESN'T DESERVE ME, ROMAN!
MAKE THEM ROW FASTER!
BONG! BONG!
BONG! BONG!
CRACK! CRACK!
STOP HAVING THOSE UNHAPPY SOULS WHIPPED, ROMAN! LOOSEN SOME OF MY BONDS! I WILL SING THEM A SONG TO LIVEN THEM UP!
?!
farewell and adieu to you fair Celtic ladies...
farewell and adieu to you ladies of Gaul...
STOP! MERCY!
WE'D RATHER HAVE THE WHIP!
CLICK! CLACK! CLONK! CLUNK! BOING!
OUR WORK ISN'T ALL FUN AND GAMES, BUT THIS IS INHUMAN! IF THE GAUL WILL SHUT UP WE PROMISE TO ROW OUR HARDEST!
YOU IGNORANT LOT! YOU BRUTES! YOU'LL ALL END UP IN THE... WELL, YOU ALREADY HAVE!
BONG.
I'M BEGINNING TO WONDER IF CAESAR REALLY DOES DESERVE THIS...
8

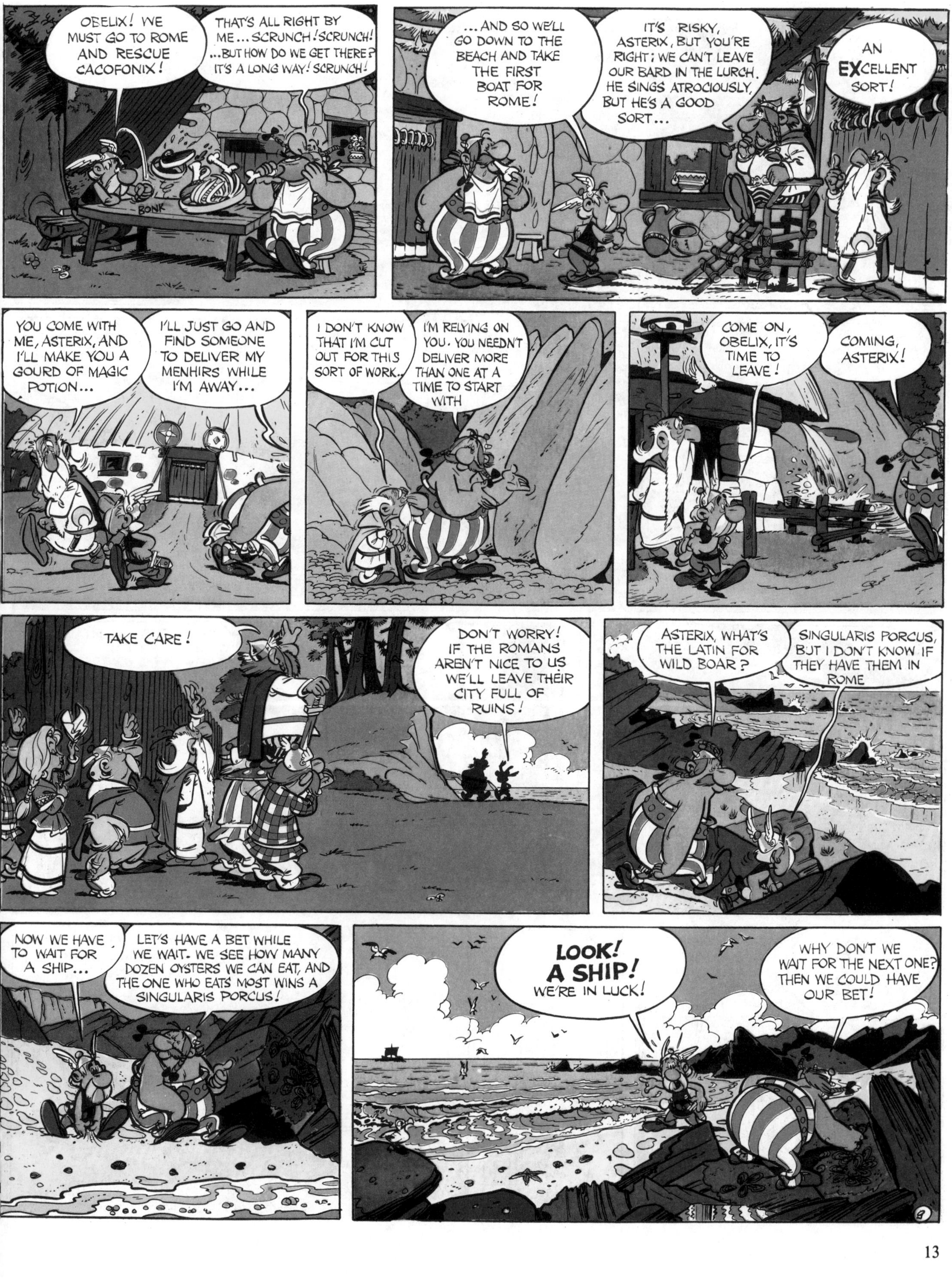
OBELIX! WE MUST GO TO ROME AND RESCUE CACOFONIX!
THAT'S ALL RIGHT BY ME... SCRUNCH! SCRUNCH! ...BUT HOW DO WE GET THERE? IT'S A LONG WAY! SCRUNCH!
BONK
...AND SO WE'LL GO DOWN TO THE BEACH AND TAKE THE FIRST BOAT FOR ROME!
IT'S RISKY, ASTERIX, BUT YOU'RE RIGHT: WE CAN'T LEAVE OUR BARD IN THE LURCH. HE SINGS ATROCIOUSLY, BUT HE'S A GOOD SORT...
AN EXCELLENT SORT!
YOU COME WITH ME, ASTERIX, AND I'LL MAKE YOU A GOURD OF MAGIC POTION...
I'LL JUST GO AND FIND SOMEONE TO DELIVER MY MENHIRS WHILE I'M AWAY...
I DON'T KNOW THAT I'M CUT OUT FOR THIS SORT OF WORK...
I'M RELYING ON YOU. YOU NEEDN'T DELIVER MORE THAN ONE AT A TIME TO START WITH
COME ON, OBELIX, IT'S TIME TO LEAVE!
COMING, ASTERIX!
TAKE CARE!
DON'T WORRY! IF THE ROMANS AREN'T NICE TO US WE'LL LEAVE THEIR CITY FULL OF RUINS!
ASTERIX, WHAT'S THE LATIN FOR WILD BOAR?
SINGULARIS PORCUS, BUT I DON'T KNOW IF THEY HAVE THEM IN ROME
NOW WE HAVE TO WAIT FOR A SHIP...
LET'S HAVE A BET WHILE WE WAIT. WE SEE HOW MANY DOZEN OYSTERS WE CAN EAT, AND THE ONE WHO EATS MOST WINS A SINGULARIS PORCUS!
LOOK! A SHIP! WE'RE IN LUCK!
WHY DON'T WE WAIT FOR THE NEXT ONE? THEN WE COULD HAVE OUR BET!

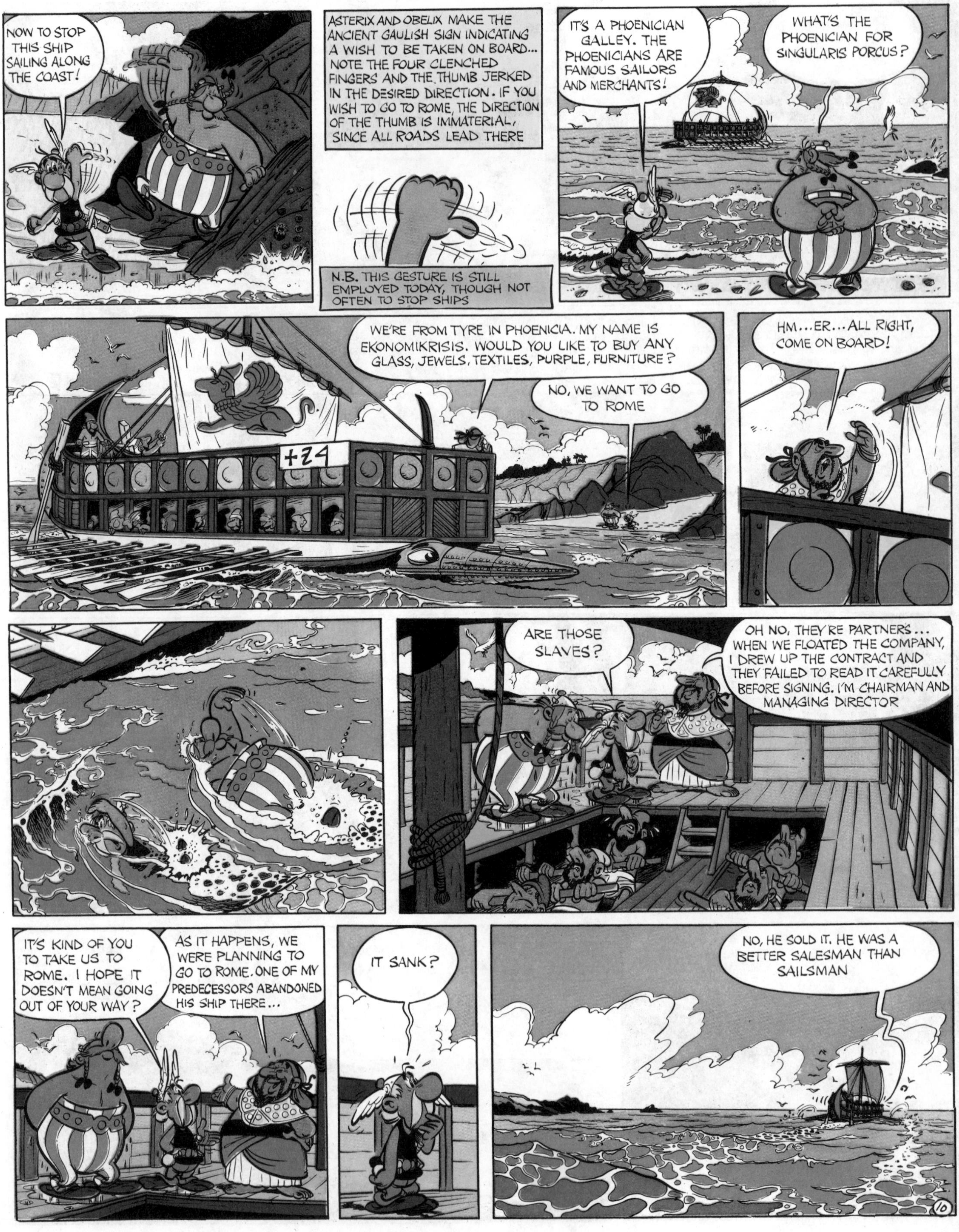
NOW TO STOP THIS SHIP SAILING ALONG THE COAST!
ASTERIX AND OBELIX MAKE THE ANCIENT GAULISH SIGN INDICATING A WISH TO BE TAKEN ON BOARD... NOTE THE FOUR CLENCHED FINGERS AND THE THUMB JERKED IN THE DESIRED DIRECTION. IF YOU WISH TO GO TO ROME, THE DIRECTION OF THE THUMB IS IMMATERIAL, SINCE ALL ROADS LEAD THERE
N.B. THIS GESTURE IS STILL EMPLOYED TODAY, THOUGH NOT OFTEN TO STOP SHIPS
IT'S A PHOENICIAN GALLEY. THE PHOENICIANS ARE FAMOUS SAILORS AND MERCHANTS!
WHAT'S THE PHOENICIAN FOR SINGULARIS PORCUS?
WE'RE FROM TYRE IN PHOENICIA. MY NAME IS EKONOMIKRISIS. WOULD YOU LIKE TO BUY ANY GLASS, JEWELS, TEXTILES, PURPLE, FURNITURE?
NO, WE WANT TO GO TO ROME
+Z4
HM...ER...ALL RIGHT, COME ON BOARD!
ARE THOSE SLAVES?
OH NO, THEY'RE PARTNERS... WHEN WE FLOATED THE COMPANY, I DREW UP THE CONTRACT AND THEY FAILED TO READ IT CAREFULLY BEFORE SIGNING. I'M CHAIRMAN AND MANAGING DIRECTOR
IT'S KIND OF YOU TO TAKE US TO ROME. I HOPE IT DOESN'T MEAN GOING OUT OF YOUR WAY?
AS IT HAPPENS, WE WERE PLANNING TO GO TO ROME. ONE OF MY PREDECESSORS ABANDONED HIS SHIP THERE...
IT SANK?
NO, HE SOLD IT. HE WAS A BETTER SALESMAN THAN SAILSMAN
10

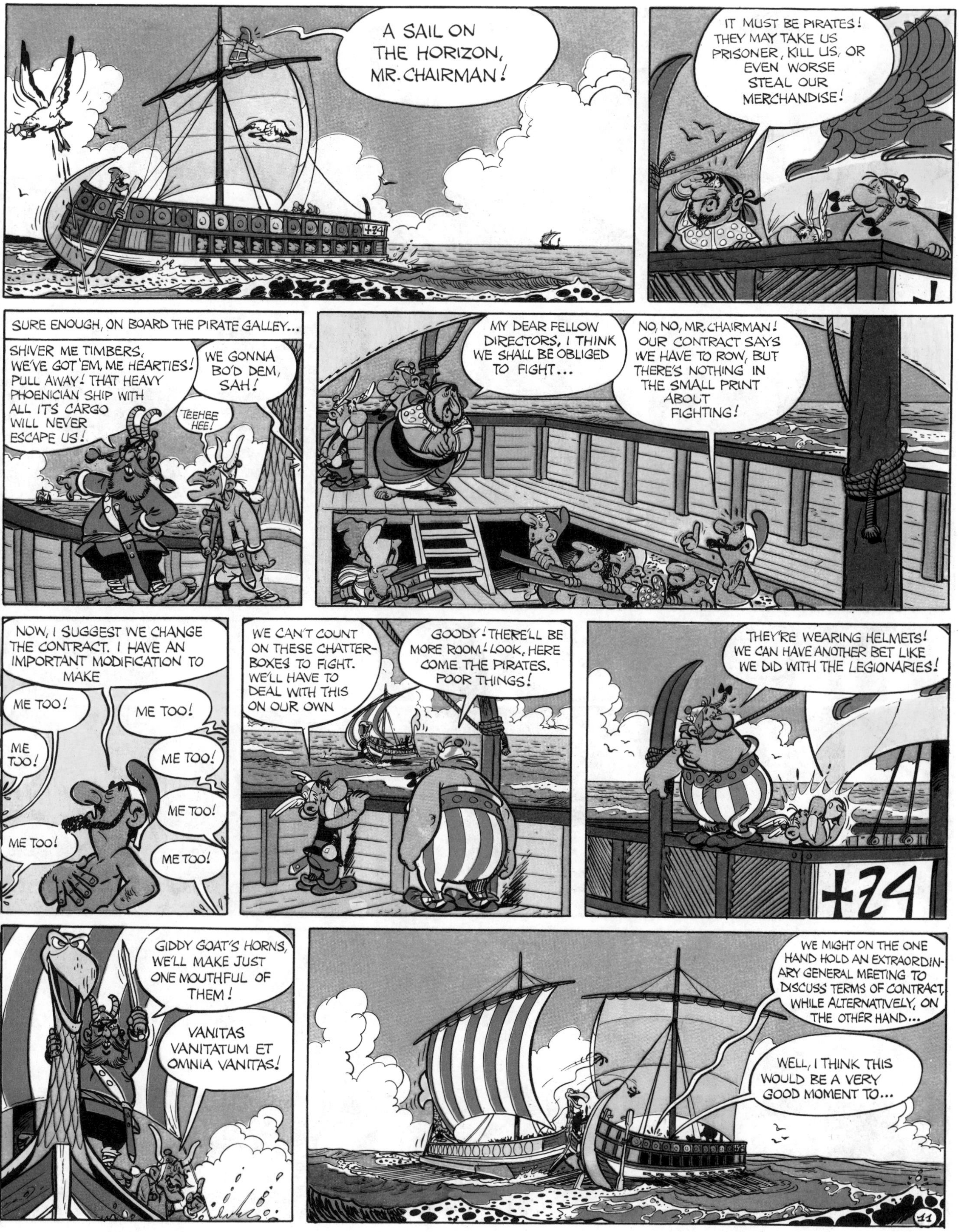

A SAIL ON THE HORIZON, MR. CHAIRMAN!
IT MUST BE PIRATES! THEY MAY TAKE US PRISONER, KILL US, OR EVEN WORSE STEAL OUR MERCHANDISE!
SURE ENOUGH, ON BOARD THE PIRATE GALLEY...
SHIVER ME TIMBERS, WE'VE GOT 'EM, ME HEARTIES! PULL AWAY! THAT HEAVY PHOENICIAN SHIP WITH ALL IT'S CARGO WILL NEVER ESCAPE US!
WE GONNA BO'D DEM, SAH!
TEEHEE HEE!
MY DEAR FELLOW DIRECTORS, I THINK WE SHALL BE OBLIGED TO FIGHT...
NO, NO, MR. CHAIRMAN! OUR CONTRACT SAYS WE HAVE TO ROW, BUT THERE'S NOTHING IN THE SMALL PRINT ABOUT FIGHTING!
NOW, I SUGGEST WE CHANGE THE CONTRACT. I HAVE AN IMPORTANT MODIFICATION TO MAKE
ME TOO!
ME TOO!
ME TOO!
ME TOO!
ME TOO!
ME TOO!
ME TOO!
WE CAN'T COUNT ON THESE CHATTER-BOXES TO FIGHT. WE'LL HAVE TO DEAL WITH THIS ON OUR OWN
GOODY! THERE'LL BE MORE ROOM! LOOK, HERE COME THE PIRATES. POOR THINGS!
THEY'RE WEARING HELMETS! WE CAN HAVE ANOTHER BET LIKE WE DID WITH THE LEGIONARIES!
GIDDY GOAT'S HORNS, WE'LL MAKE JUST ONE MOUTHFUL OF THEM!
VANITAS VANITATUM ET OMNIA VANITAS!
WE MIGHT ON THE ONE HAND HOLD AN EXTRAORDIN-ARY GENERAL MEETING TO DISCUSS TERMS OF CONTRACT, WHILE ALTERNATIVELY, ON THE OTHER HAND...
WELL, I THINK THIS WOULD BE A VERY GOOD MOMENT TO...
11

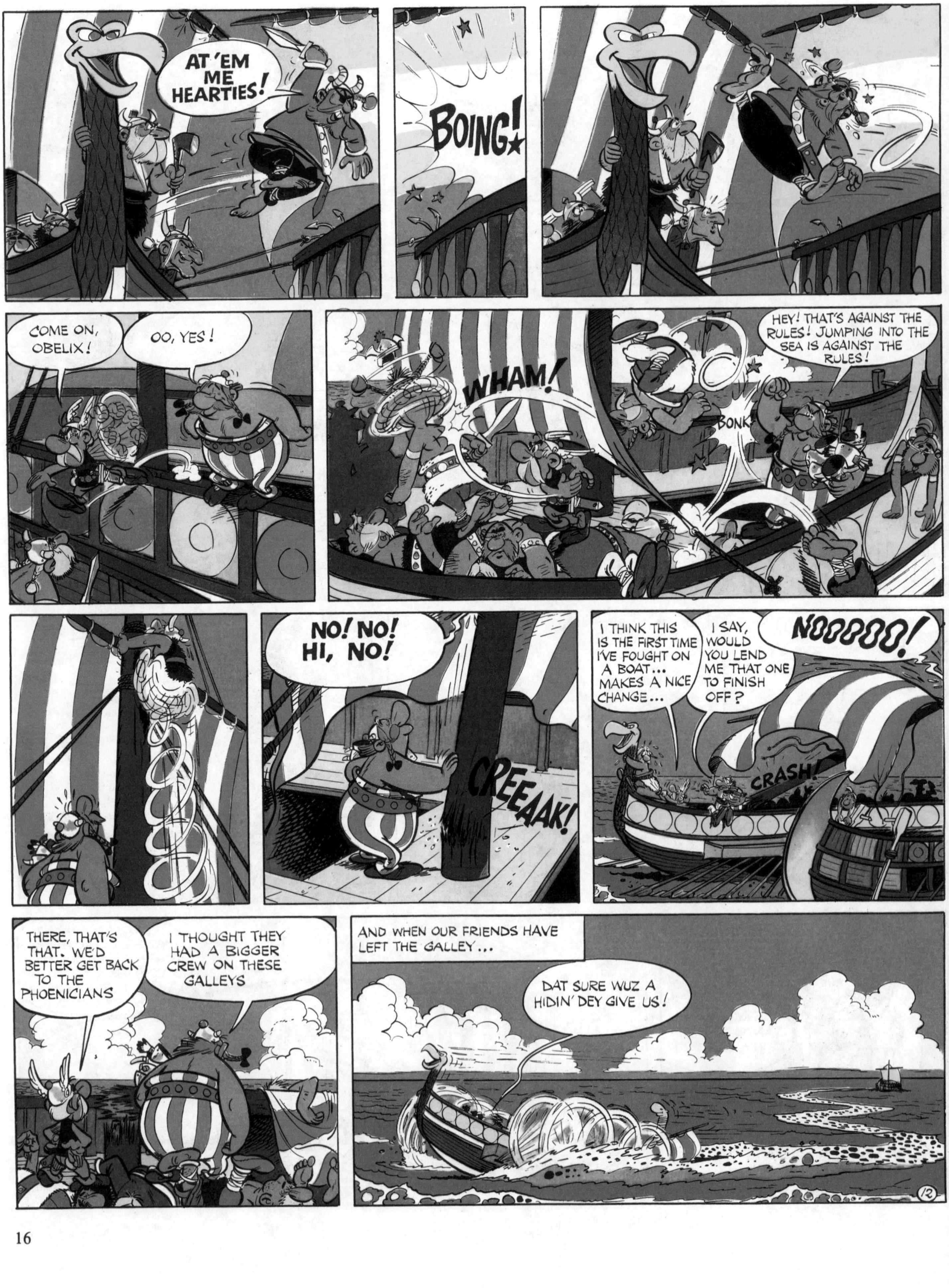
AT'EM ME HEARTIES!
BOING!
COME ON, OBELIX!
OO, YES!
WHAM!
HEY! THAT'S AGAINST THE RULES! JUMPING INTO THE SEA IS AGAINST THE RULES!
BONK
NO! NO! HI, NO!
CREEAAK!
I THINK THIS IS THE FIRST TIME I'VE FOUGHT ON A BOAT... MAKES A NICE CHANGE...
I SAY, WOULD YOU LEND ME THAT ONE TO FINISH OFF?
NOOOOO!
CRASH!
THERE, THAT'S THAT. WE'D BETTER GET BACK TO THE PHOENICIANS
I THOUGHT THEY HAD A BIGGER CREW ON THESE GALLEYS
AND WHEN OUR FRIENDS HAVE LEFT THE GALLEY...
DAT SURE WUZ A HIDIN' DEY GIVE US!
12

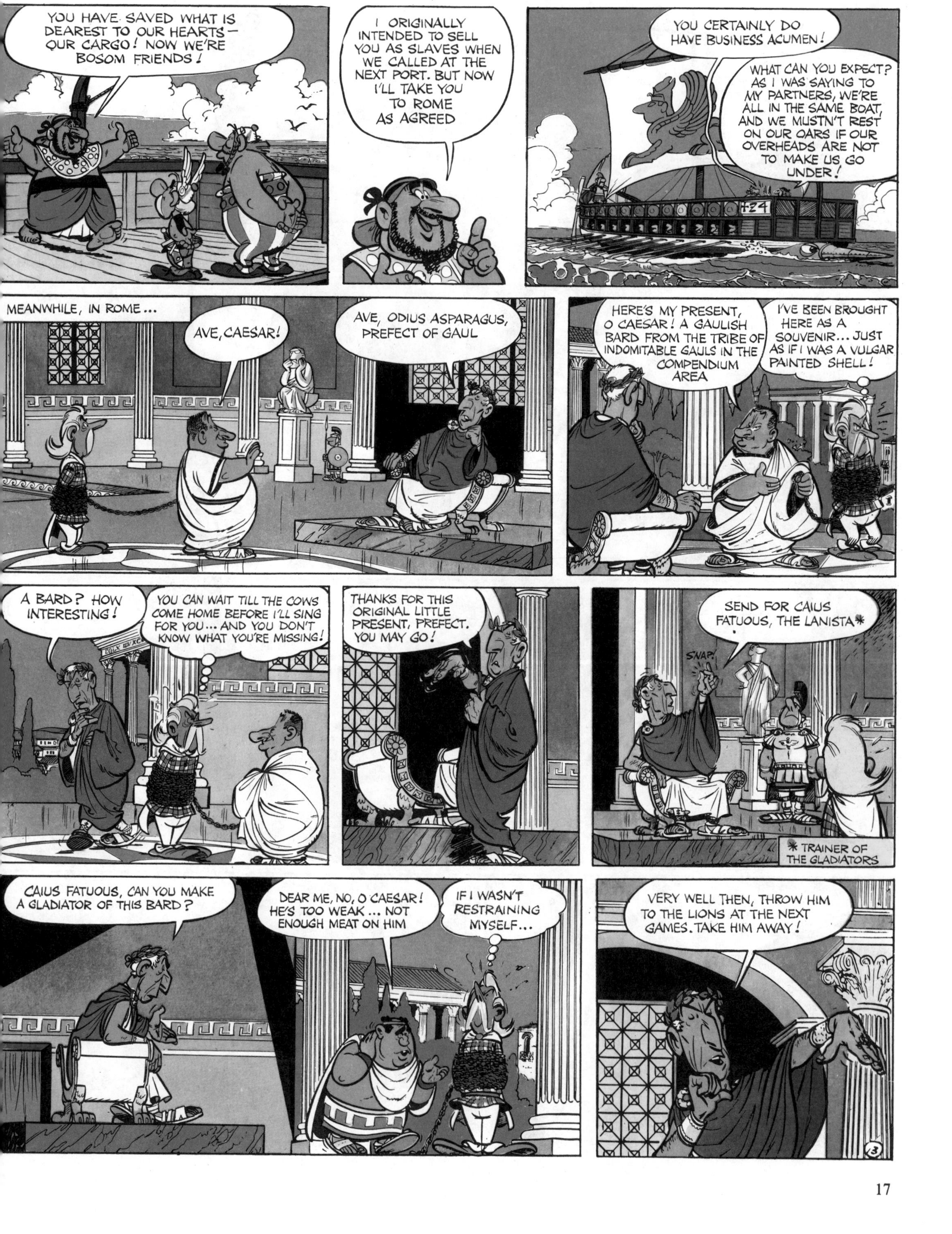
YOU HAVE SAVED WHAT IS DEAREST TO OUR HEARTS — OUR CARGO! NOW WE'RE BOSOM FRIENDS!
I ORIGINALLY INTENDED TO SELL YOU AS SLAVES WHEN WE CALLED AT THE NEXT PORT. BUT NOW I'LL TAKE YOU TO ROME AS AGREED
YOU CERTAINLY DO HAVE BUSINESS ACUMEN!
WHAT CAN YOU EXPECT? AS I WAS SAYING TO MY PARTNERS, WE'RE ALL IN THE SAME BOAT, AND WE MUSTN'T REST ON OUR OARS IF OUR OVERHEADS ARE NOT TO MAKE US GO UNDER!
MEANWHILE, IN ROME...
AVE, CAESAR!
AVE, ODIUS ASPARAGUS, PREFECT OF GAUL
HERE'S MY PRESENT, O CAESAR! A GAULISH BARD FROM THE TRIBE OF INDOMITABLE GAULS IN THE COMPENDIUM AREA
I'VE BEEN BROUGHT HERE AS A SOUVENIR... JUST AS IF I WAS A VULGAR PAINTED SHELL!
A BARD? HOW INTERESTING!
YOU CAN WAIT TILL THE COWS COME HOME BEFORE I'LL SING FOR YOU... AND YOU DON'T KNOW WHAT YOU'RE MISSING!
THANKS FOR THIS ORIGINAL LITTLE PRESENT, PREFECT. YOU MAY GO!
SNAP!
SEND FOR CAIUS FATUOUS, THE LANISTA*.
* TRAINER OF THE GLADIATORS
CAIUS FATUOUS, CAN YOU MAKE A GLADIATOR OF THIS BARD?
DEAR ME, NO, O CAESAR! HE'S TOO WEAK... NOT ENOUGH MEAT ON HIM
IF I WASN'T RESTRAINING MYSELF...
VERY WELL THEN, THROW HIM TO THE LIONS AT THE NEXT GAMES. TAKE HIM AWAY!

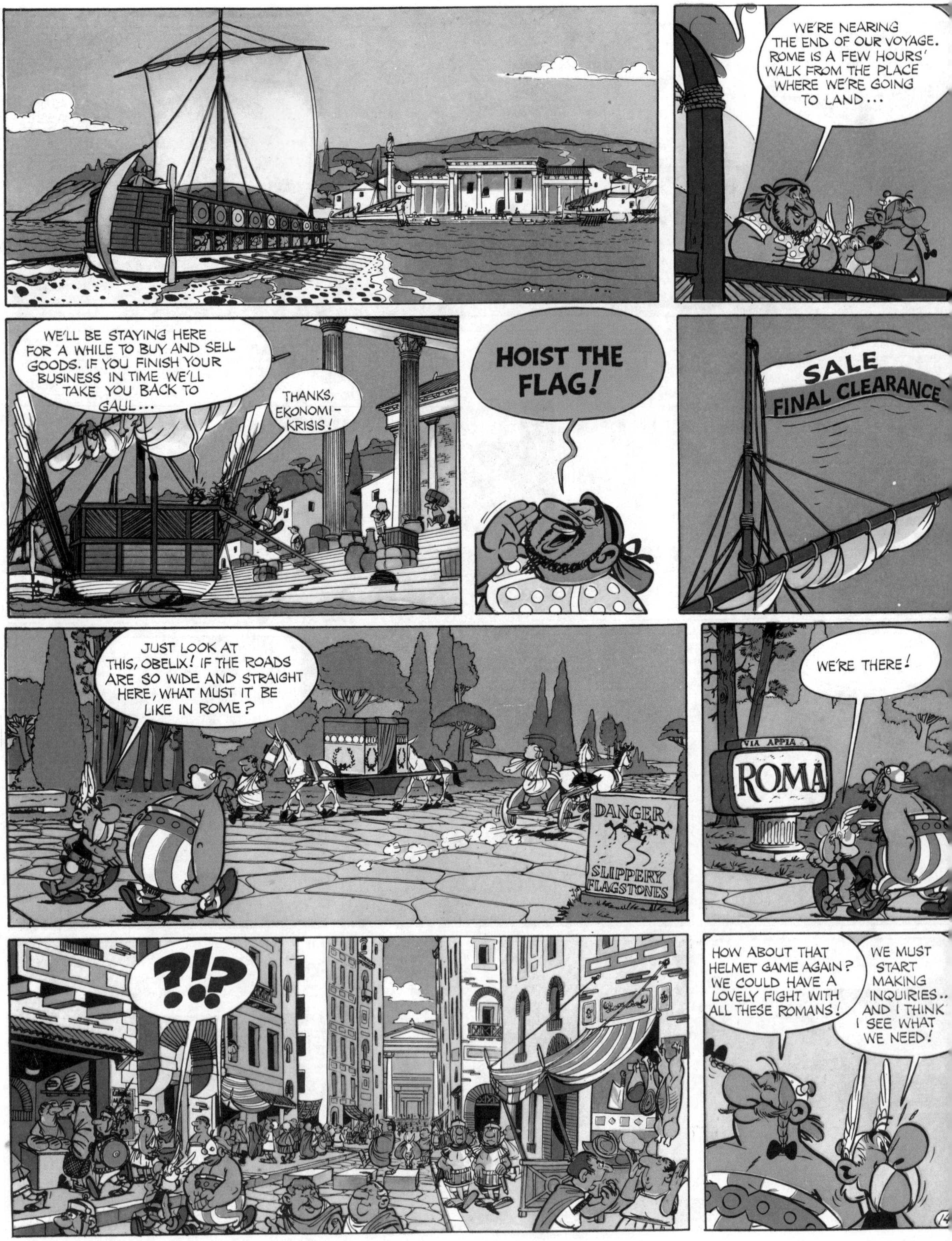

WE'RE NEARING THE END OF OUR VOYAGE. ROME IS A FEW HOURS' WALK FROM THE PLACE WHERE WE'RE GOING TO LAND...
WE'LL BE STAYING HERE FOR A WHILE TO BUY AND SELL GOODS. IF YOU FINISH YOUR BUSINESS IN TIME WE'LL TAKE YOU BACK TO GAUL...
THANKS, EKONOMIKRISIS!
HOIST THE FLAG!
SALE
FINAL CLEARANCE
JUST LOOK AT THIS, OBELIX! IF THE ROADS ARE SO WIDE AND STRAIGHT HERE, WHAT MUST IT BE LIKE IN ROME?
DANGER
SLIPPERY FLAGSTONES
WE'RE THERE!
VIA APPIA
ROMA
?!?
HOW ABOUT THAT HELMET GAME AGAIN? WE COULD HAVE A LOVELY FIGHT WITH ALL THESE ROMANS!
WE MUST START MAKING INQUIRIES.. AND I THINK I SEE WHAT WE NEED!

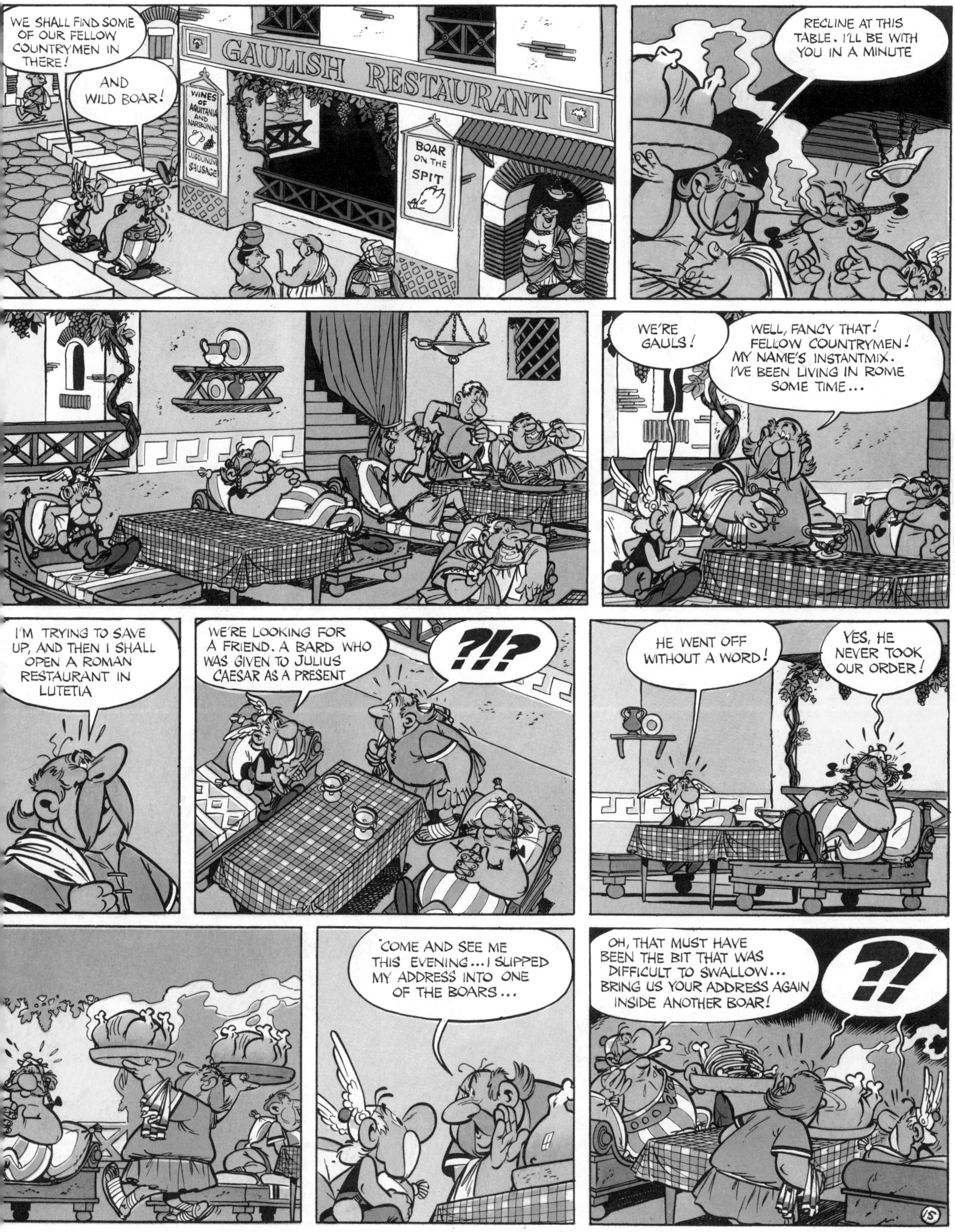

WE SHALL FIND SOME OF OUR FELLOW COUNTRYMEN IN THERE!
AND WILD BOAR!
GAULISH RESTAURANT
WINES OF AQUITANIA AND NARBONNE
LUGDUNUM SAUSAGE
BOAR ON THE SPIT
RECLINE AT THIS TABLE. I'LL BE WITH YOU IN A MINUTE
WE'RE GAULS!
WELL, FANCY THAT! FELLOW COUNTRYMEN! MY NAME'S INSTANTMIX. I'VE BEEN LIVING IN ROME SOME TIME...
I'M TRYING TO SAVE UP, AND THEN I SHALL OPEN A ROMAN RESTAURANT IN LUTETIA
WE'RE LOOKING FOR A FRIEND. A BARD WHO WAS GIVEN TO JULIUS CAESAR AS A PRESENT
?!?
HE WENT OFF WITHOUT A WORD!
YES, HE NEVER TOOK OUR ORDER!
COME AND SEE ME THIS EVENING... I SLIPPED MY ADDRESS INTO ONE OF THE BOARS...
OH, THAT MUST HAVE BEEN THE BIT THAT WAS DIFFICULT TO SWALLOW... BRING US YOUR ADDRESS AGAIN INSIDE ANOTHER BOAR!
?!
15

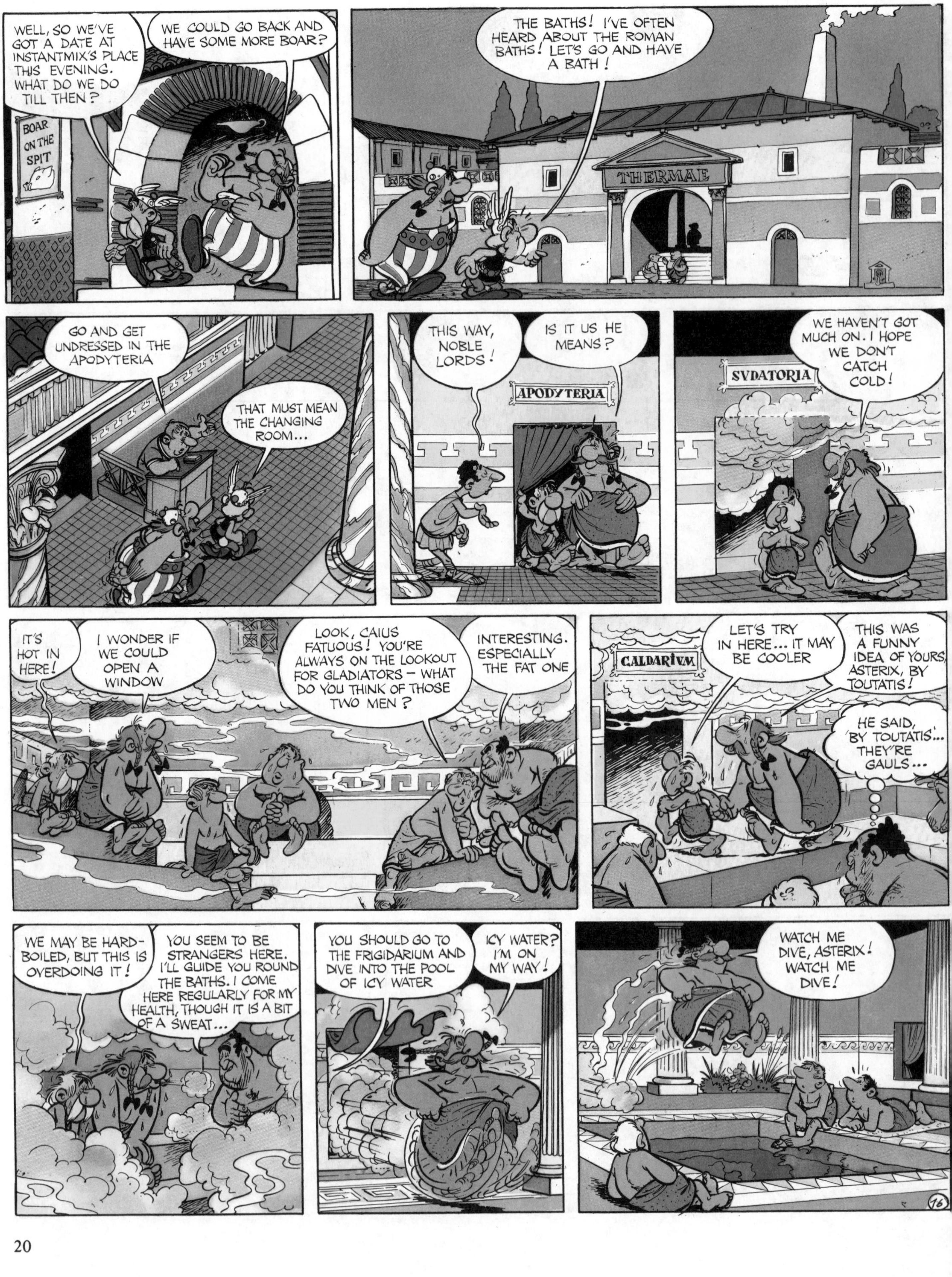

WELL, SO WE'VE GOT A DATE AT INSTANTMIX'S PLACE THIS EVENING. WHAT DO WE DO TILL THEN?
WE COULD GO BACK AND HAVE SOME MORE BOAR?
BOAR ON THE SPIT
THE BATHS! I'VE OFTEN HEARD ABOUT THE ROMAN BATHS! LET'S GO AND HAVE A BATH!
THERMAE
GO AND GET UNDRESSED IN THE APODYTERIA
THAT MUST MEAN THE CHANGING ROOM...
THIS WAY, NOBLE LORDS!
IS IT US HE MEANS?
APODYTERIA
SVDATORIA
WE HAVEN'T GOT MUCH ON. I HOPE WE DON'T CATCH COLD!
IT'S HOT IN HERE!
I WONDER IF WE COULD OPEN A WINDOW
LOOK, CAIUS FATUOUS! YOU'RE ALWAYS ON THE LOOKOUT FOR GLADIATORS – WHAT DO YOU THINK OF THOSE TWO MEN?
INTERESTING. ESPECIALLY THE FAT ONE
CALDARIVM
LET'S TRY IN HERE... IT MAY BE COOLER
THIS WAS A FUNNY IDEA OF YOURS, ASTERIX, BY TOUTATIS!
HE SAID, 'BY TOUTATIS'... THEY'RE GAULS...
WE MAY BE HARD-BOILED, BUT THIS IS OVERDOING IT!
YOU SEEM TO BE STRANGERS HERE. I'LL GUIDE YOU ROUND THE BATHS. I COME HERE REGULARLY FOR MY HEALTH, THOUGH IT IS A BIT OF A SWEAT...
YOU SHOULD GO TO THE FRIGIDARIUM AND DIVE INTO THE POOL OF ICY WATER
ICY WATER? I'M ON MY WAY!
WATCH ME DIVE, ASTERIX! WATCH ME DIVE!
16

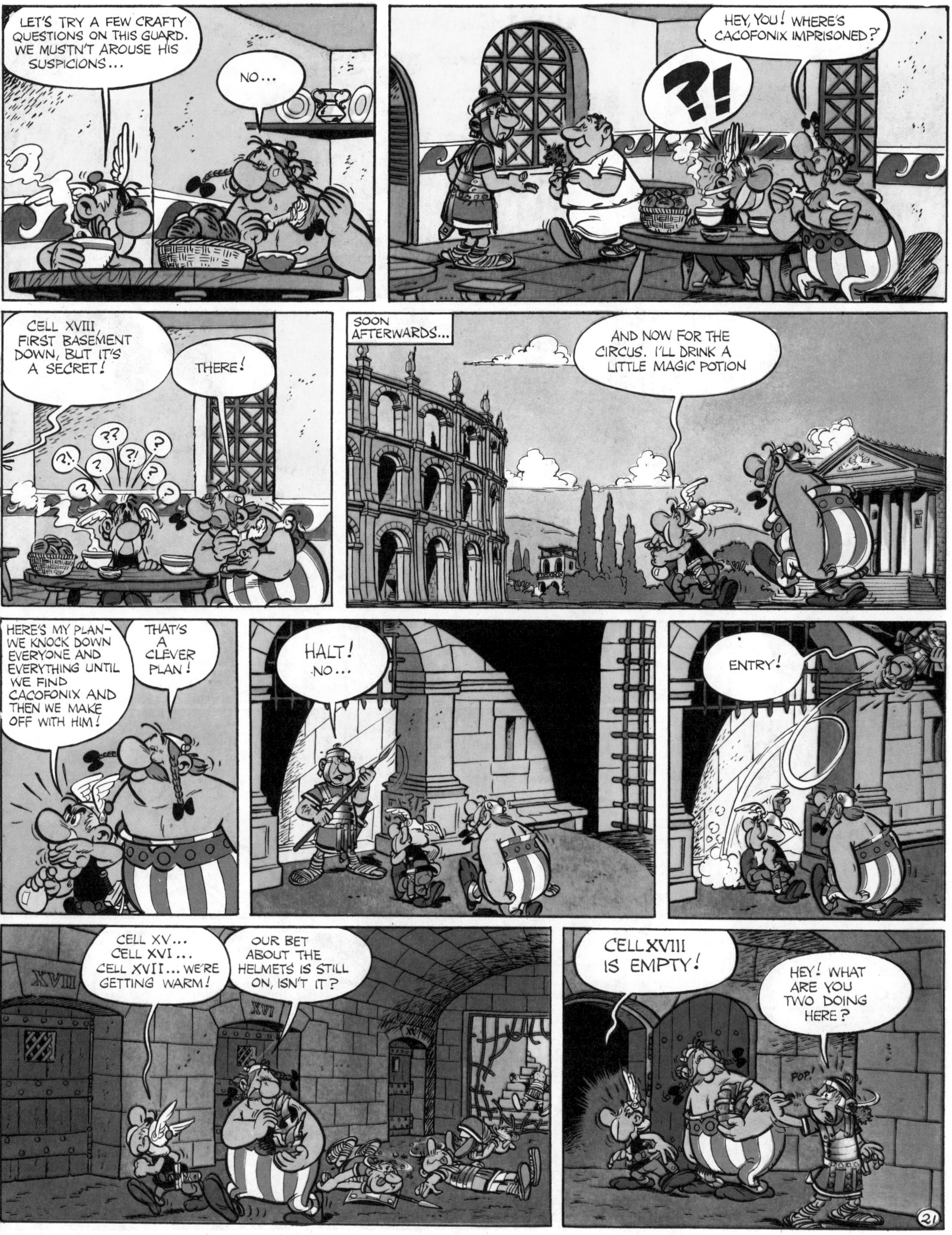
LET'S TRY A FEW CRAFTY QUESTIONS ON THIS GUARD. WE MUSTN'T AROUSE HIS SUSPICIONS...
NO...
HEY, YOU! WHERE'S CACOFONIX IMPRISONED?
?!
CELL XVIII FIRST BASEMENT DOWN, BUT IT'S A SECRET!
THERE!
SOON AFTERWARDS...
AND NOW FOR THE CIRCUS. I'LL DRINK A LITTLE MAGIC POTION
HERE'S MY PLAN– WE KNOCK DOWN EVERYONE AND EVERYTHING UNTIL WE FIND CACOFONIX AND THEN WE MAKE OFF WITH HIM!
THAT'S A CLEVER PLAN!
HALT! NO...
ENTRY!
CELL XV... CELL XVI... CELL XVII... WE'RE GETTING WARM!
OUR BET ABOUT THE HELMETS IS STILL ON, ISN'T IT?
XVII
XVI
CELL XVIII IS EMPTY!
HEY! WHAT ARE YOU TWO DOING HERE?
POP!
21

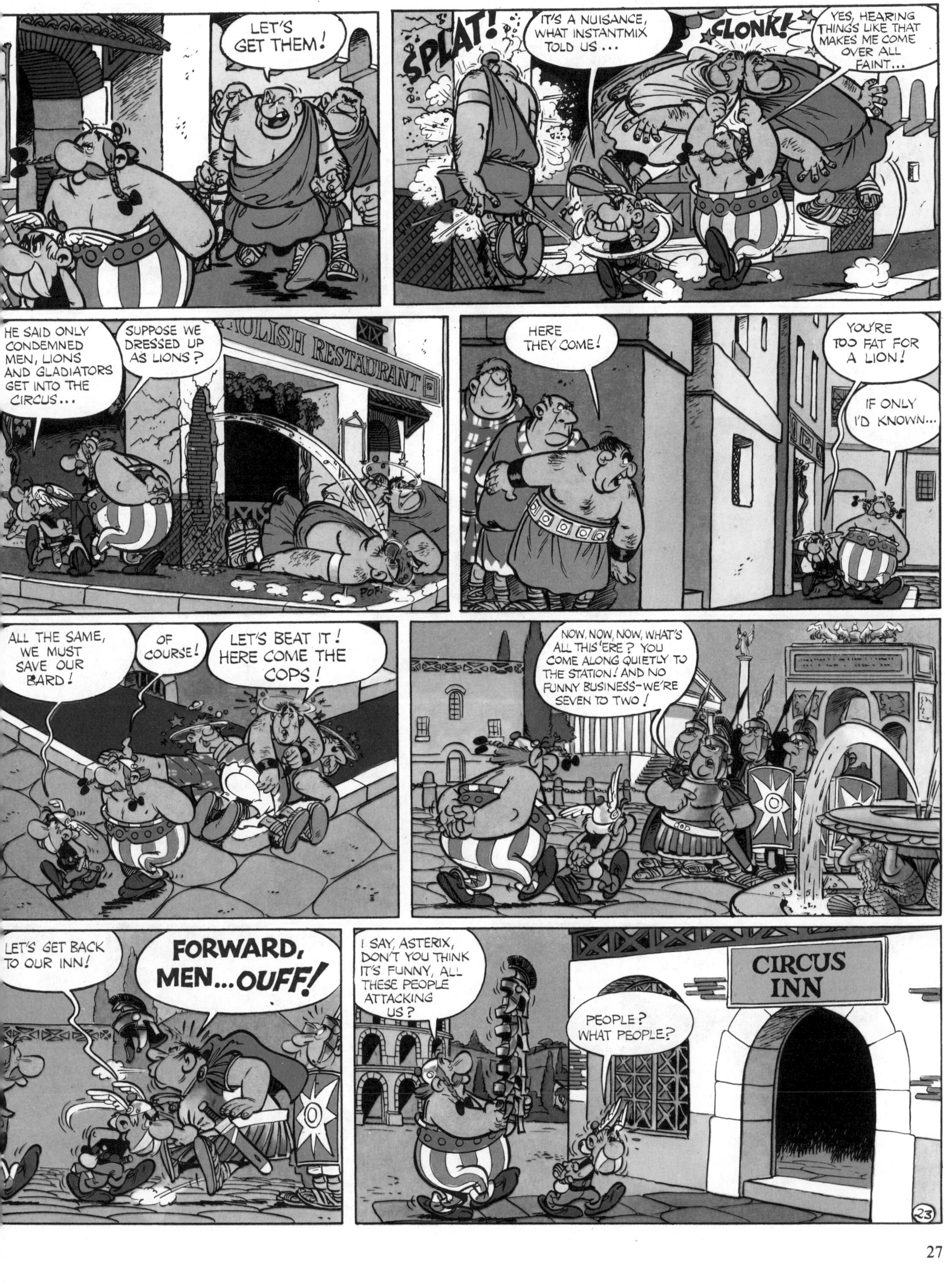

LET'S GET THEM!
SPLAT!
IT'S A NUISANCE, WHAT INSTANTMIX TOLD US...
CLONK!
YES, HEARING THINGS LIKE THAT MAKES ME COME OVER ALL FAINT...
HE SAID ONLY CONDEMNED MEN, LIONS AND GLADIATORS GET INTO THE CIRCUS...
SUPPOSE WE DRESSED UP AS LIONS?
HERE THEY COME!
YOU'RE TOO FAT FOR A LION!
IF ONLY I'D KNOWN...
ALL THE SAME, WE MUST SAVE OUR BARD!
OF COURSE!
LET'S BEAT IT! HERE COME THE COPS!
NOW, NOW, NOW, WHAT'S ALL THIS 'ERE? YOU COME ALONG QUIETLY TO THE STATION! AND NO FUNNY BUSINESS–WE'RE SEVEN TO TWO!
LET'S GET BACK TO OUR INN!
FORWARD, MEN...OUFF!
I SAY, ASTERIX, DON'T YOU THINK IT'S FUNNY, ALL THESE PEOPLE ATTACKING US?
CIRCUS INN
PEOPLE? WHAT PEOPLE?
23

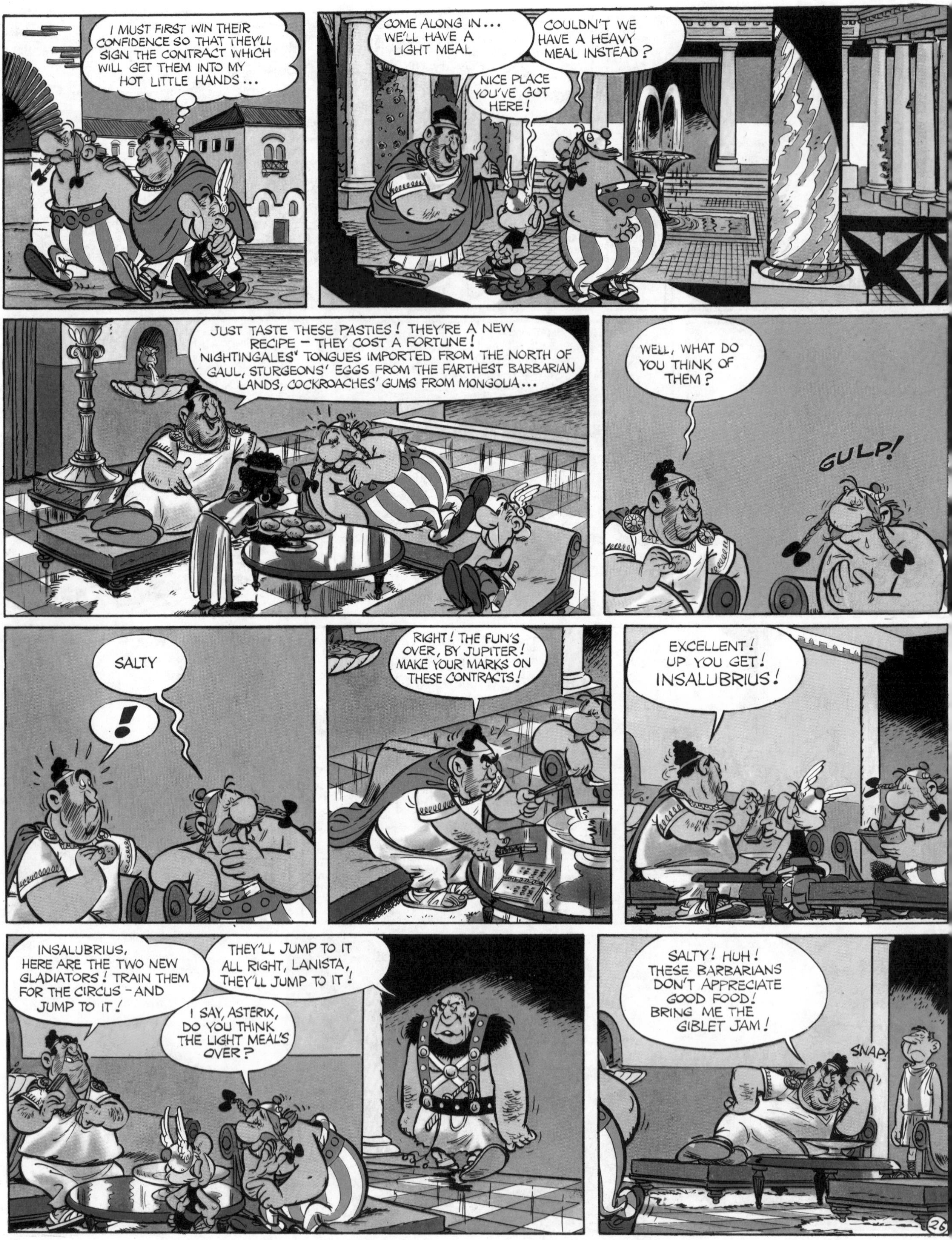
I MUST FIRST WIN THEIR CONFIDENCE SO THAT THEY'LL SIGN THE CONTRACT WHICH WILL GET THEM INTO MY HOT LITTLE HANDS...
COME ALONG IN... WE'LL HAVE A LIGHT MEAL
NICE PLACE YOU'VE GOT HERE!
COULDN'T WE HAVE A HEAVY MEAL INSTEAD?
JUST TASTE THESE PASTIES! THEY'RE A NEW RECIPE – THEY COST A FORTUNE! NIGHTINGALES' TONGUES IMPORTED FROM THE NORTH OF GAUL, STURGEONS' EGGS FROM THE FARTHEST BARBARIAN LANDS, COCKROACHES' GUMS FROM MONGOLIA...
WELL, WHAT DO YOU THINK OF THEM?
GULP!
SALTY
!
RIGHT! THE FUN'S OVER, BY JUPITER! MAKE YOUR MARKS ON THESE CONTRACTS!
EXCELLENT! UP YOU GET! INSALUBRIUS!
INSALUBRIUS, HERE ARE THE TWO NEW GLADIATORS! TRAIN THEM FOR THE CIRCUS – AND JUMP TO IT!
THEY'LL JUMP TO IT ALL RIGHT, LANISTA, THEY'LL JUMP TO IT!
I SAY, ASTERIX, DO YOU THINK THE LIGHT MEAL'S OVER?
SALTY! HUH! THESE BARBARIANS DON'T APPRECIATE GOOD FOOD! BRING ME THE GIBLET JAM!
SNAP!
26

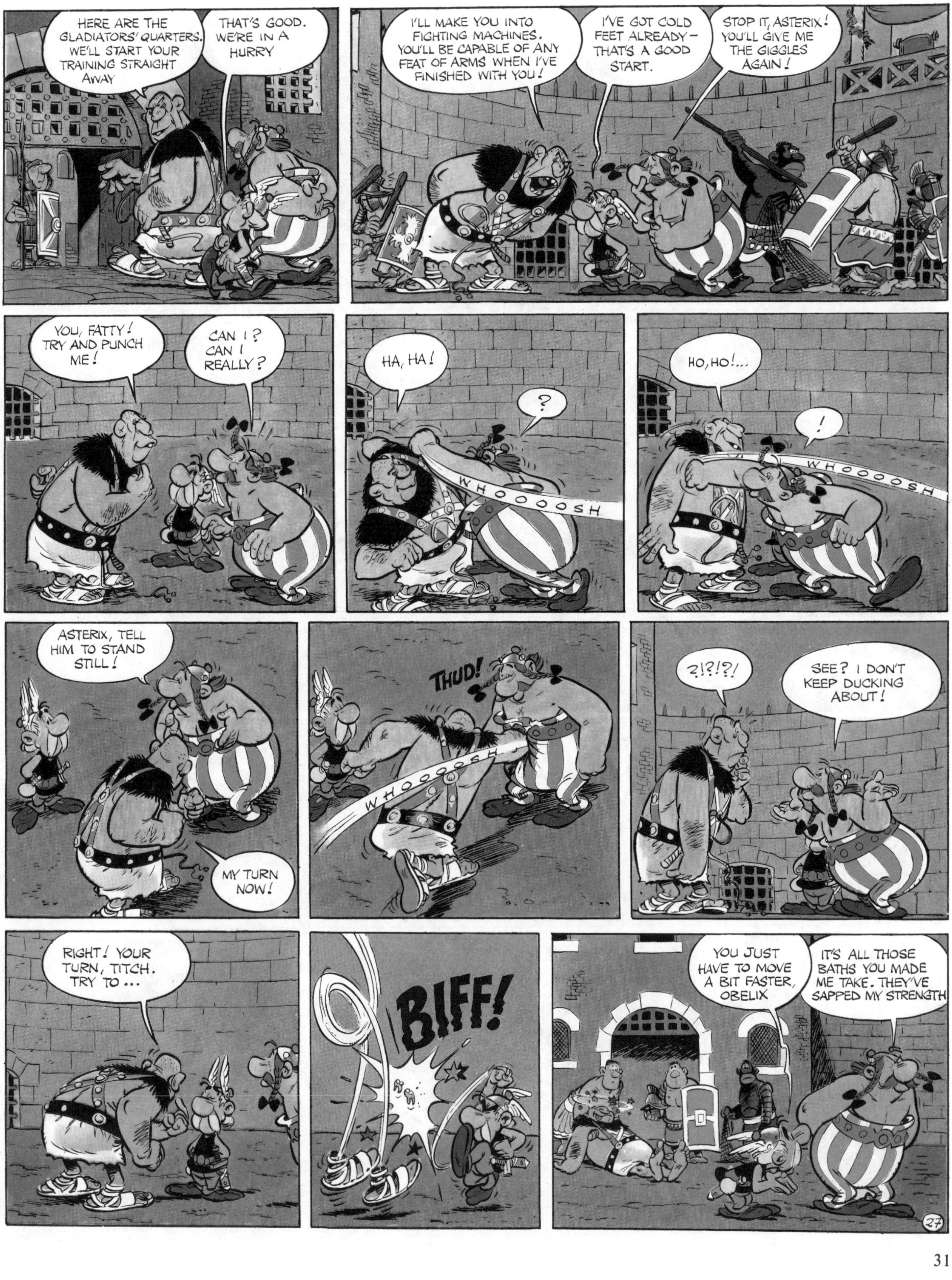
HERE ARE THE GLADIATORS' QUARTERS. WE'LL START YOUR TRAINING STRAIGHT AWAY
THAT'S GOOD. WE'RE IN A HURRY
I'LL MAKE YOU INTO FIGHTING MACHINES. YOU'LL BE CAPABLE OF ANY FEAT OF ARMS WHEN I'VE FINISHED WITH YOU!
I'VE GOT COLD FEET ALREADY – THAT'S A GOOD START.
STOP IT, ASTERIX! YOU'LL GIVE ME THE GIGGLES AGAIN!
YOU, FATTY! TRY AND PUNCH ME!
CAN I? CAN I REALLY?
HA, HA!
?
WHOOOOOSH
HO, HO!...
!
WHOOOOOSH
ASTERIX, TELL HIM TO STAND STILL!
MY TURN NOW!
THUD!
WHOOOOOSH
?!?!?!
SEE? I DON'T KEEP DUCKING ABOUT!
RIGHT! YOUR TURN, TITCH. TRY TO ...
BIFF!
YOU JUST HAVE TO MOVE A BIT FASTER, OBELIX
IT'S ALL THOSE BATHS YOU MADE ME TAKE. THEY'VE SAPPED MY STRENGTH
27

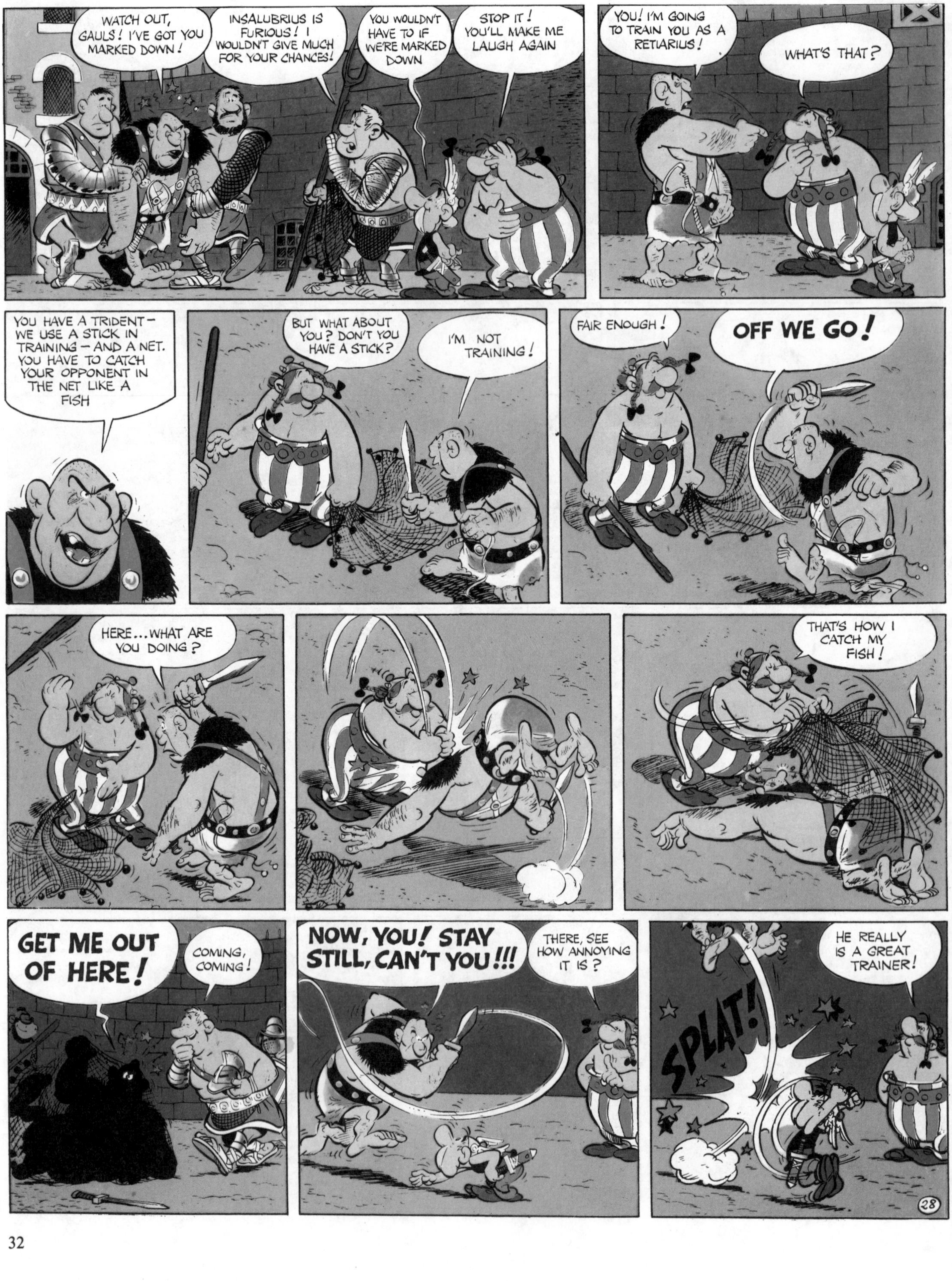

WATCH OUT, GAULS! I'VE GOT YOU MARKED DOWN!
INSALUBRIUS IS FURIOUS! I WOULDN'T GIVE MUCH FOR YOUR CHANCES!
YOU WOULDN'T HAVE TO IF WE'RE MARKED DOWN
STOP IT! YOU'LL MAKE ME LAUGH AGAIN
YOU! I'M GOING TO TRAIN YOU AS A RETIARIUS!
WHAT'S THAT?
YOU HAVE A TRIDENT— WE USE A STICK IN TRAINING—AND A NET. YOU HAVE TO CATCH YOUR OPPONENT IN THE NET LIKE A FISH
BUT WHAT ABOUT YOU? DON'T YOU HAVE A STICK?
I'M NOT TRAINING!
FAIR ENOUGH!
OFF WE GO!
HERE...WHAT ARE YOU DOING?
THAT'S HOW I CATCH MY FISH!
GET ME OUT OF HERE!
COMING, COMING!
NOW, YOU! STAY STILL, CAN'T YOU!!!
THERE, SEE HOW ANNOYING IT IS?
SPLAT!
HE REALLY IS A GREAT TRAINER!
28

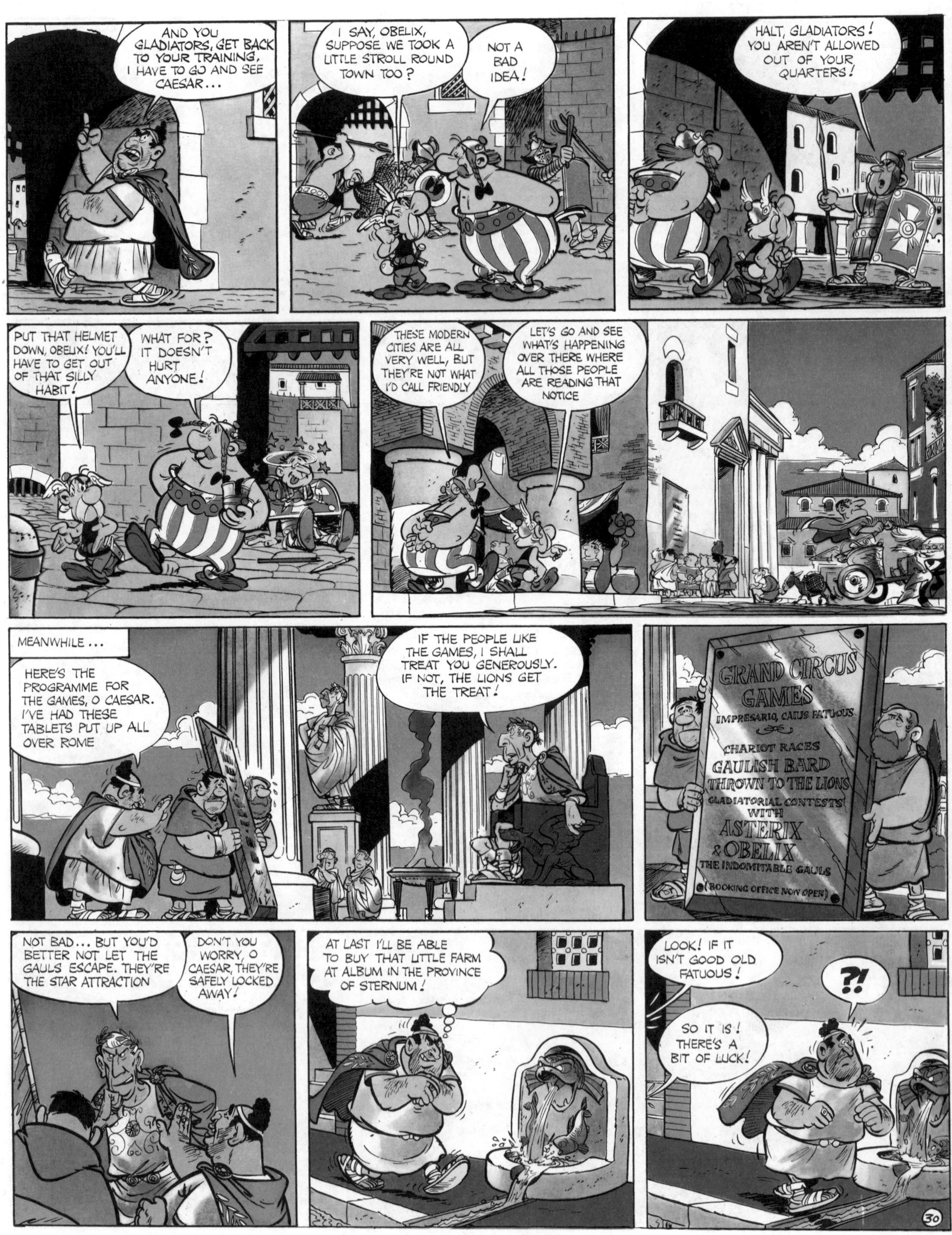
AND YOU GLADIATORS, GET BACK TO YOUR TRAINING, I HAVE TO GO AND SEE CAESAR...
I SAY, OBELIX, SUPPOSE WE TOOK A LITTLE STROLL ROUND TOWN TOO?
NOT A BAD IDEA!
HALT, GLADIATORS! YOU AREN'T ALLOWED OUT OF YOUR QUARTERS!
PUT THAT HELMET DOWN, OBELIX! YOU'LL HAVE TO GET OUT OF THAT SILLY HABIT!
WHAT FOR? IT DOESN'T HURT ANYONE!
THESE MODERN CITIES ARE ALL VERY WELL, BUT THEY'RE NOT WHAT I'D CALL FRIENDLY
LET'S GO AND SEE WHAT'S HAPPENING OVER THERE WHERE ALL THOSE PEOPLE ARE READING THAT NOTICE
MEANWHILE...
HERE'S THE PROGRAMME FOR THE GAMES, O CAESAR. I'VE HAD THESE TABLETS PUT UP ALL OVER ROME
IF THE PEOPLE LIKE THE GAMES, I SHALL TREAT YOU GENEROUSLY. IF NOT, THE LIONS GET THE TREAT!
GRAND CIRCUS GAMES
IMPRESARIO, CAIUS FATUOUS
CHARIOT RACES
GAULISH BARD THROWN TO THE LIONS
GLADIATORIAL CONTESTS WITH ASTERIX & OBELIX THE INDOMITABLE GAULS
(BOOKING OFFICE NOW OPEN)
NOT BAD... BUT YOU'D BETTER NOT LET THE GAULS ESCAPE. THEY'RE THE STAR ATTRACTION
DON'T YOU WORRY, O CAESAR, THEY'RE SAFELY LOCKED AWAY!
AT LAST I'LL BE ABLE TO BUY THAT LITTLE FARM AT ALBUM IN THE PROVINCE OF STERNUM!
LOOK! IF IT ISN'T GOOD OLD FATUOUS!
?!
SO IT IS! THERE'S A BIT OF LUCK!
30

TIME PASSES BY, AND THE GLADIATORS ARE PUTTING ON WEIGHT...

MY FIRST IS A HUNDRED, MY SECOND IS A SIGN OF THE ZODIAC, MY THIRD IS A HIBERNIAN, MY FOURTH IS THE EGYPTIAN GOD OF THE SUN AND JULIUS CAESAR LOVES MY WHOLE! WHO AM I?

WHILE CAIUS FATUOUS IS LOSING IT...

THERE THEY GO AGAIN! PLAYING IDIOTIC GAMES INSTEAD OF TRAINING! A FINE CIRCUS THIS IS GOING TO BE!

IT'S C, LEO, PAT, RA... CLEOPATRA!

THAT WAS A DIFFICULT ONE THAT WAS!

THE GAMES ARE FIXED FOR TOMORROW. THIS WILL BE YOUR LAST NIGHT IN THE CIRCUS, YOU USELESS LOT!

WE DON'T REALLY WANT TO FIGHT ANY MORE, ASTERIX

DON'T WORRY! I PROMISE YOU WON'T HAVE TO RISK YOUR LIVES IN THE ARENA!

AND A VERY RELAXED GROUP OF GLADIATORS ARRIVES AT THE CIRCUS...

HA, HA! HO, HO!

STOP PUSHING, WILL YOU!

PORPUS IS A BEAST! PASS IT ON!

WHAT'S THE MATTER WITH THEM?

NO IDEA. LOCK THEM UP DOWN BELOW!

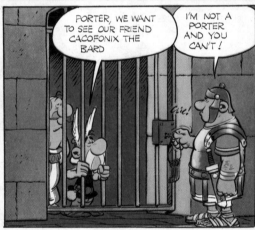

PORTER, WE WANT TO SEE OUR FRIEND CACOFONIX THE BARD

I'M NOT A PORTER AND YOU CAN'T!

VERY WELL THEN, WE SHALL TEAR OUT THESE BARS ONE BY ONE UNTIL YOU CO-OPERATE!

GO AHEAD AND TRY!

PLINNNK!

PLONNNK!

PLUNNNK!

STOP! LEAVE THE FIXTURES ALONE!

AH, ABOUT TIME TOO! WHAT SERVICE!

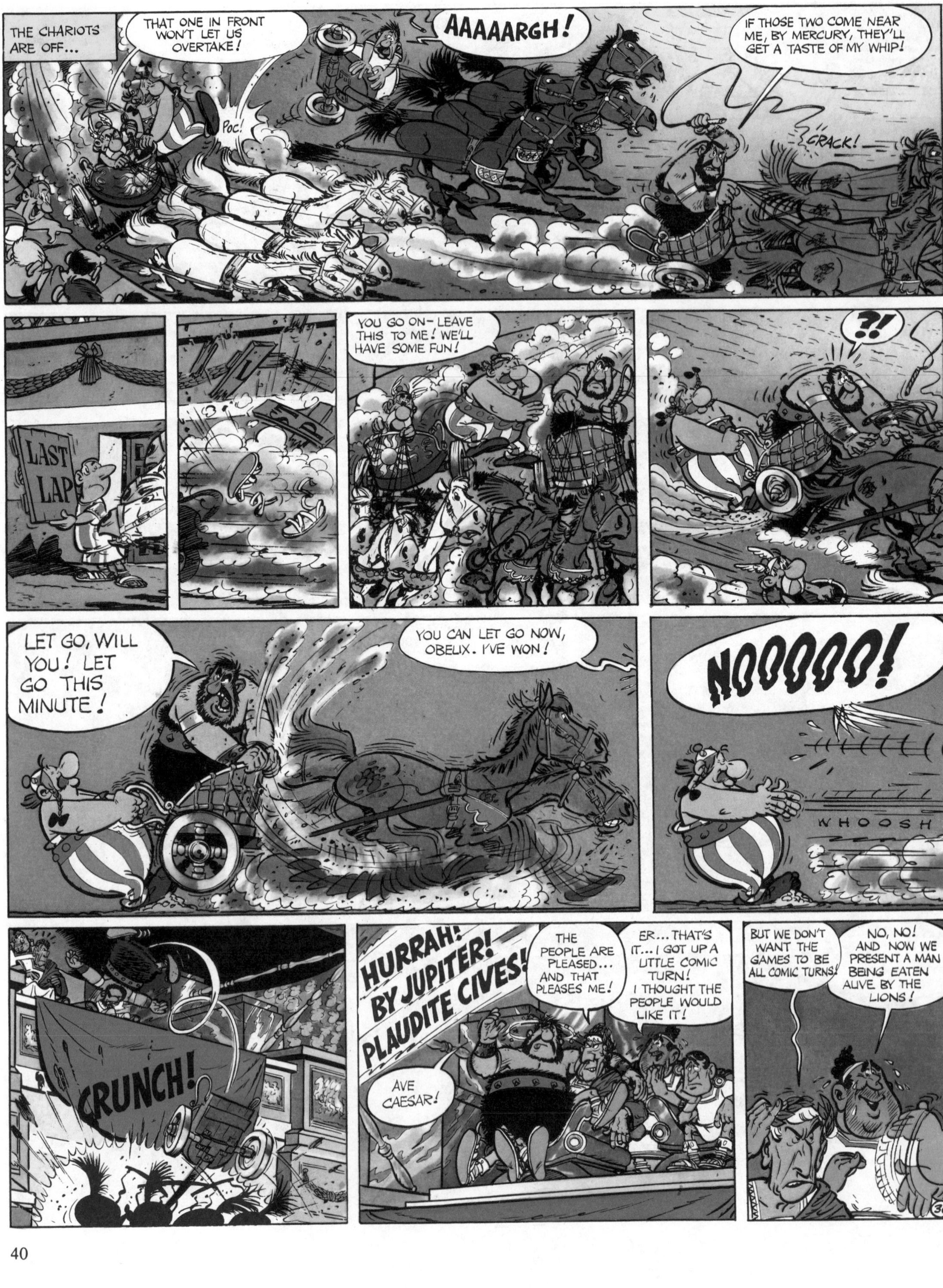

THE CHARIOTS ARE OFF...
THAT ONE IN FRONT WON'T LET US OVERTAKE!
Poc!
AAAAARGH!
IF THOSE TWO COME NEAR ME, BY MERCURY, THEY'LL GET A TASTE OF MY WHIP!
CRACK!
LAST LAP
YOU GO ON– LEAVE THIS TO ME! WE'LL HAVE SOME FUN!
?!
LET GO, WILL YOU! LET GO THIS MINUTE!
YOU CAN LET GO NOW, OBELIX. I'VE WON!
NOOOOO!
WHOOSH
CRUNCH!
HURRAH! BY JUPITER! PLAUDITE CIVES!
AVE CAESAR!
THE PEOPLE ARE PLEASED... AND THAT PLEASES ME!
ER... THAT'S IT... I GOT UP A LITTLE COMIC TURN! I THOUGHT THE PEOPLE WOULD LIKE IT!
BUT WE DON'T WANT THE GAMES TO BE ALL COMIC TURNS!
NO, NO! AND NOW WE PRESENT A MAN BEING EATEN ALIVE BY THE LIONS!
36

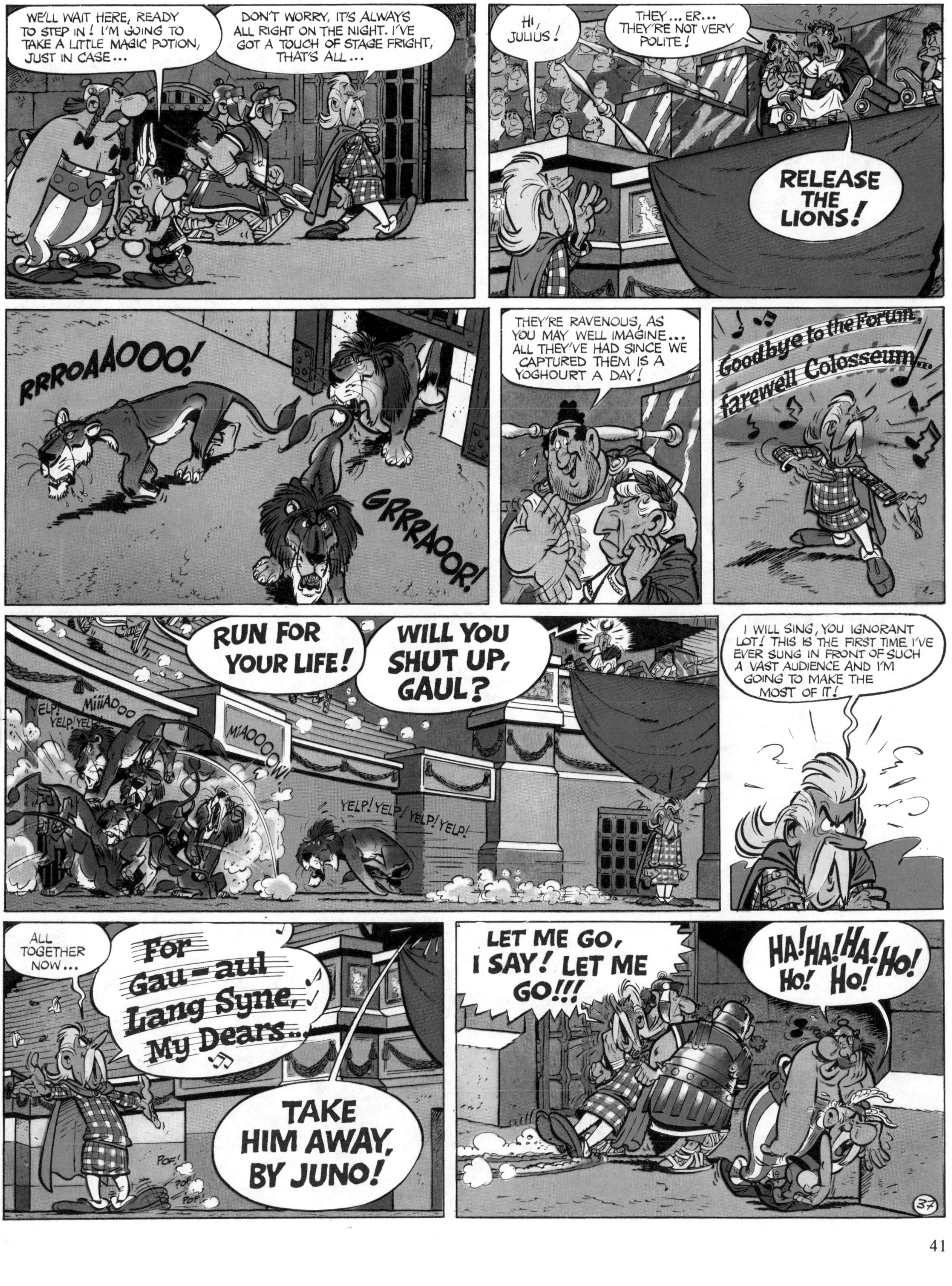
WE'LL WAIT HERE, READY TO STEP IN! I'M GOING TO TAKE A LITTLE MAGIC POTION, JUST IN CASE...
DON'T WORRY, IT'S ALWAYS ALL RIGHT ON THE NIGHT. I'VE GOT A TOUCH OF STAGE FRIGHT, THAT'S ALL...
HI, JULIUS!
THEY... ER... THEY'RE NOT VERY POLITE!
RELEASE THE LIONS!
RRROAAOOO!
GRRRAOOR!
THEY'RE RAVENOUS, AS YOU MAY WELL IMAGINE... ALL THEY'VE HAD SINCE WE CAPTURED THEM IS A YOGHOURT A DAY!
Goodbye to the Forum, farewell Colosseum...
RUN FOR YOUR LIFE!
WILL YOU SHUT UP, GAUL?
YELP! YELP! YELP!
MiiiAOOO
MiAOOOOW!
YELP! YELP! YELP! YELP!
I WILL SING, YOU IGNORANT LOT! THIS IS THE FIRST TIME I'VE EVER SUNG IN FRONT OF SUCH A VAST AUDIENCE AND I'M GOING TO MAKE THE MOST OF IT!
ALL TOGETHER NOW...
For Gau-aul Lang Syne, My Dears...
TAKE HIM AWAY, BY JUNO!
POF!
POF!
POF!
LET ME GO, I SAY! LET ME GO!!!
HA! HA! HA! HA! Ho! Ho! Ho!
37

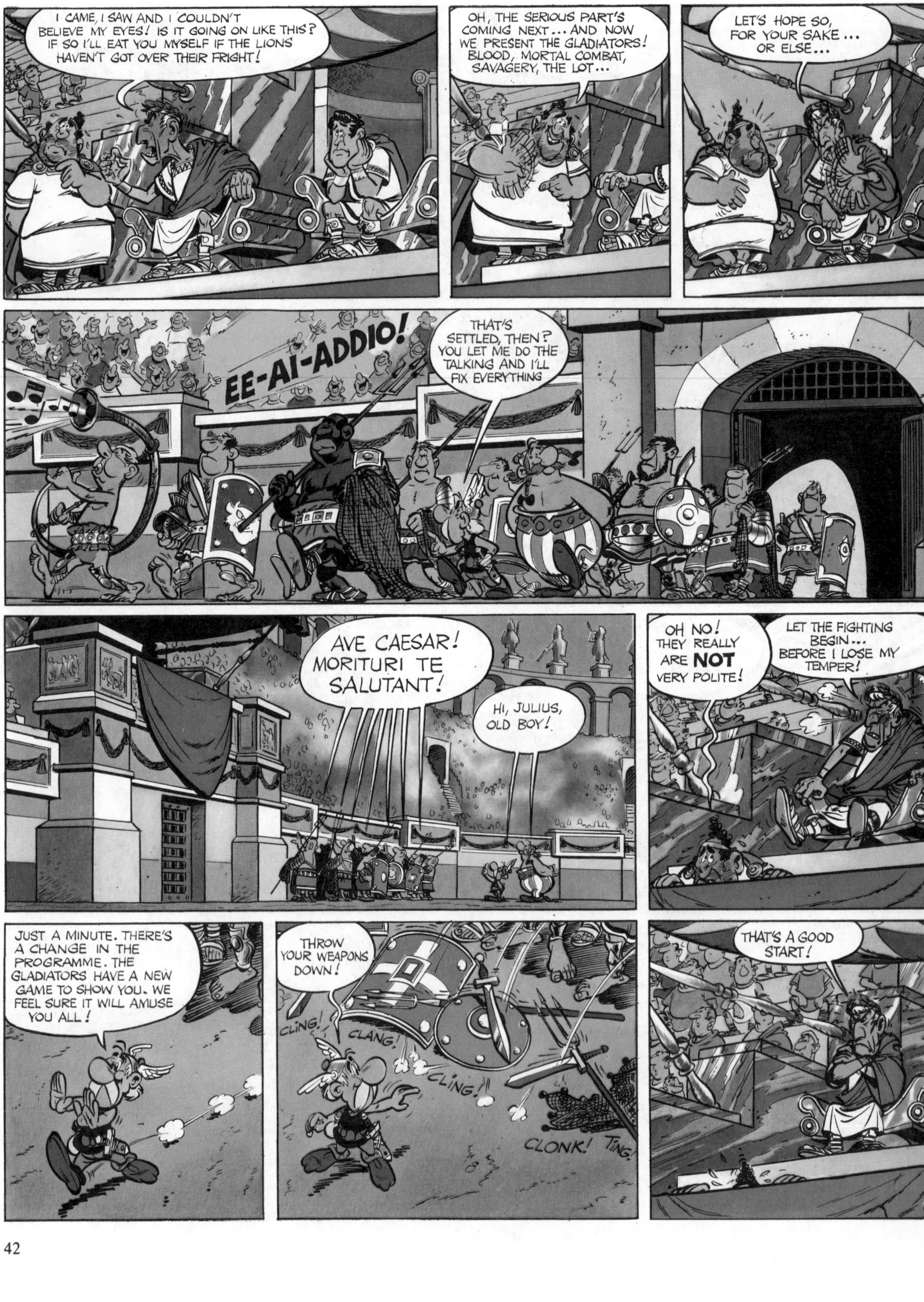
I CAME, I SAW AND I COULDN'T BELIEVE MY EYES! IS IT GOING ON LIKE THIS? IF SO I'LL EAT YOU MYSELF IF THE LIONS HAVEN'T GOT OVER THEIR FRIGHT!
OH, THE SERIOUS PART'S COMING NEXT... AND NOW WE PRESENT THE GLADIATORS! BLOOD, MORTAL COMBAT, SAVAGERY, THE LOT...
LET'S HOPE SO, FOR YOUR SAKE... OR ELSE...
EE-AI-ADDIO!
THAT'S SETTLED, THEN? YOU LET ME DO THE TALKING AND I'LL FIX EVERYTHING
AVE CAESAR! MORITURI TE SALUTANT!
HI, JULIUS, OLD BOY!
OH NO! THEY REALLY ARE **NOT** VERY POLITE!
LET THE FIGHTING BEGIN... BEFORE I LOSE MY TEMPER!
JUST A MINUTE. THERE'S A CHANGE IN THE PROGRAMME. THE GLADIATORS HAVE A NEW GAME TO SHOW YOU. WE FEEL SURE IT WILL AMUSE YOU ALL!
THROW YOUR WEAPONS DOWN!
CLING!
CLANG!
CLING!
CLONK!
TING!
THAT'S A GOOD START!
38